STEVEN GRAY

DEATH COMES TO ROCK SPRINGS

Complete and Unabridged

LINFORD
Leicester

First published in Great Britain in 1996 by
Robert Hale Limited
London

First Linford Edition
published 1997
by arrangement with
Robert Hale Limited
London

British Library CIP Data

Gray, Steven
    Death comes to Rock Springs.—Large print ed.—
    Linford western library
    1. Western stories
    2. Large type books
    I. Title
    823.9'14 [F]

    ISBN 0–7089–5052–3

Published by
F. A. Thorpe (Publishing) Ltd.
Anstey, Leicestershire

Set by Words & Graphics Ltd.
Anstey, Leicestershire
Printed and bound in Great Britain by
T. J. Press (Padstow) Ltd., Padstow, Cornwall

This book is printed on acid-free paper

1

THE rocky overhang didn't provide much protection. Driven by the wind, rain swirled in and dripped from a crack somewhere up above. It had been raining since early morning, turning the ground into mud, although at long last a break had appeared in the scudding clouds; a lighter grey amongst the dark overcast.

Jarrod Kilkline sat, hunched miserably, on his horse. He stared out at the flat, soaking earth that swept away to the distant mountains. Nothing and no one moved out there.

He was wet through. His leg ached from the wound gained in the last months of the war, as it always did when the weather was cold or wet. And he hadn't eaten anything since the morning of the day before, when, passing through a small town, he'd cadged some bread and coffee from the motherly waitress at the cafe.

He felt light headed, feverish. A long way from both his home in Georgia and the deserts of Southern Arizona where he'd ended up after the Civil War. But he was safe in neither home nor Arizona. In Georgia he was in trouble with the army for the shooting and killing of a Union army soldier, and in Arizona he was wanted by the law for the robbery of several stagecoaches down near Tucson.[1] A bounty hunter, skilled in tracking and shooting, was on his trail. He'd seen no sign of the man for the past couple of weeks but that didn't mean he wasn't out there somewhere.

Not far off now was the border with Utah, to which he was fleeing, hoping to find sanctuary with the Mormons.

---

[1] See *Rebels Forever*

But the rest of the journey wasn't going to be easy, taking him into the mountains, the slopes of which were still snowclad this early in the year. He needed warm clothing and food, and soon. And as he had no money and nothing to trade, he had only one way to get what he needed. He would have to steal it.

Once, before the war, even during it, Jarrod would never have considered stealing anything from anyone. Now that he was a wanted outlaw, with a price on his head, stealing food and clothes to keep himself alive didn't really seem all that much of a crime.

That was why he waited here under the overhang; not just for its dubious shelter but in the hope that some time soon someone would pass by on their way into town from one of the outlying farms dotting the valley.

Jarrod too was a farmer by upbringing and inclination and it was to run the family farm that he had returned to Georgia after the Civil War. It hadn't worked out like that and now he doubted whether he could ever become a farmer or return home again.

* * *

Lester Peabody was glad when the town came into view. He was wet, cold and cross. Now it had stopped raining, a number of citizens had emerged onto the streets. He was aware of them looking at him curiously, some of the less mannered actually laughing. He ignored them. Out here, everywhere he went, people considered him an Eastern greenhorn; at least until they got to know him. Then they took him very seriously indeed.

Wanting to get business underway before finding a place to stay and a barber's where he could be shaved and enjoy a bath, he headed first for the Marshal's office.

Marshal Pollard looked up as the door opened and his visitor came in.

He almost smiled.

The stranger was in his thirties, of middle height and slim build, with dark brown hair, slicked back with grease, and a ruddy complexion made all the redder by the western sun. He carried a derby hat and, under his yellow slicker, wore a vividly checked suit and shoes — shoes, goddammit! He carried no weapon by his side, which, even in this farming community, was most unusual.

"What can I do for you?"

"Lester Peabody." Peabody reached out a hand for the marshal to shake and wasting no more time put a piece of paper down on the desk. It was a Wanted poster. "Have you seen this man?"

"Jarrod Kilkline?" Pollard picked up the poster to study it. It showed a drawing of a young man, about twenty-five, with dark hair straggling to his shoulders.

"He's tall and thin," Peabody added. "With wary eyes and a limp from a wound received in the war. He's also got a Southern, Georgian, accent."

"Hmm, you know I think I did see someone like that. Just the other day." The Marshal scratched his head. "Yeah, yesterday morning. Before it started to rain."

Peabody smiled widely. "Good. Is he still around?"

"I doubt it. He didn't look like he had enough money to rent a room in the boarding house and there wasn't anyone sleeping in the stables when I did my rounds this morning."

"What about the saloon or a brothel?"

"This is a respectable town, Mr Peabody. We've got a saloon but all it does is sell drinks. We ain't got no whores." The Marshal paused. "Are you a lawman?"

"No."

"Then what do you want with him?"

"I'm not interested in the shooting of the soldier in Georgia. That's army business. I'm after him for his part in several stagecoach robberies last year.

Him and another fellow called Harry Phillips were involved."

The Marshal noted that Peabody avoided mentioning the word 'bounty-hunter', although that was undoubtedly what he was.

"This man was alone."

"Yes, I know. Him and Phillips had a falling out. To be honest, Phillips was the real wrong-un. Kilkline was fooled into going along with the robberies because he believed they were raising money to start up another war."

Pollard nodded. Not that he really understood. The Civil War had taken place hundreds of miles away. He couldn't figure out what it was that made brother fight brother over a principle.

"But Kilkline's got to pay for what he did and right now I know where he is. Once I've got him then I'll set about finding Phillips."

"You seem very sure of yourself."

"I'm employed by Edgar Thorndike of Tucson who runs the stagecoach line and I don't intend to let him down."

Peabody left the office in a much better frame of mind than he'd entered it. At last — he was catching up with Jarrod Kilkline.

He'd been on his trail since just after Christmas. For a while he'd been in danger of losing him. That had been the fault of that Sergeant who'd let Kilkline go — just because he'd helped a green lieutenant and his foolish girlfriend in their escapades with the Apaches — and then he'd prevented Peabody from going after him.[1] Peabody hadn't liked that. He didn't appreciate his own failure.

Now it seemed he was only a couple of days behind his quarry.

★ ★ ★

_____
[1] See *Renegade Range*

The rain gradually stopped and a shaft of pale sunlight touched the sky. At the same time Jarrod heard the sound of a horse's plodding hooves, accompanied by the creak of badly oiled wheels. He peered out from the rocks and swore. Preoccupied with his own misery, he hadn't been listening out. The buckboard was almost on top of him; would soon be past.

Jarrod pulled his pistol from its holster, and digging heels into his horse's side, urged it forward.

Two people sat huddled together on the buckboard's seat, trying to keep dry and warm under a piece of tarpaulin pulled over their heads. A farmer and his wife. Both in their fifties, with greying hair and lined faces.

By the time they saw him, Jarrod was in the middle of the road. Pointing his gun at them, he said, "Hold it right there."

"What the hell?" the man said while

the woman cried out, "William, be careful."

"I mean you no harm," Jarrod said, as the man, cursing, drew the pony to a halt.

They sat watching him, the man scowling, the woman with an anxious look on her face.

"What do you want?" William asked.

"Your slicker and jacket for a start." Jarrod was relieved to see that the man wore thick clothes and that, as he was tall and reasonably broad, they would fit all right; be too big in fact. "Then any money and food you've got with you."

"And if I refuse?"

"I'll be forced to use this." Jarrod raised his pistol.

"Thought you didn't mean us no harm."

"Oh, William, do as he says!"

"Yeah, it would be best. I really don't want to hurt you." Jarrod rode forward as William stood up beginning to take off his jacket. There was a rifle in the back of the buckboard and Jarrod took hold of it, throwing it down on the ground, out of the man's reach.

"Here!" William flung the jacket and slicker at him.

"And the money."

"We don't have much," the woman said.

"Right now my need is greater than your's."

She opened her purse and took out a small cloth bag. Its contents rattled as she handed it over to Jarrod so he thought it was mostly coins, with perhaps a couple of bills. But anything was better than nothing.

"Any food in there?"

"Of course there ain't," William snarled. "That's why we're going to town, to buy some. Or at least we were. Now what the hell are we going to do?"

"It doesn't matter," his wife caught hold of his arm, pulling him back down.

11

"I'm real sorry about this," Jarrod said. He slid the bag into one of the saddlebags and held the clothes in front of him. "Sorry," he repeated and without looking back, fearing that if he did he'd give back what he'd stolen, he rode away.

* * *

Peabody heard the commotion before he saw it. He went to the window of his rented room, which overlooked the street. A buckboard had pulled up outside the Marshal's office, with a man and woman on the seat. The man, wearing only shirt and trousers, was shouting, "We've been robbed! Marshal!" Quickly other men and women began to gather round.

Peabody was smaller than most of the men in the crowd but somehow that didn't stop him bulling his way to the front.

By this time, the woman was being comforted by several friends while the man was raving at Marshal Pollard.

"He wanted my clothes! He took our money!"

Robbery was unusual around here and seeing Lester Peabody, Marshal Pollard felt sure this had something to do with the young man the bounty hunter was after. What was his name? Ah yes, Jarrod Kilkline.

"I want him caught. He's a dangerous outlaw!"

"Oh, William, he wasn't," his wife protested, tears in her eyes. "He was polite and apologized for what he had to do. I felt sorry for him."

Most of the men present grunted, thinking only a woman could say something like that!

"I would gladly have given him money and food had he but asked."

"He did ask," William said. "At the point of a damn gun!"

"What did he look like?" Peabody asked. He too had no doubt that the thief was Kilkline but it was always wise to make sure.

"Young, tall, thin. Long dark hair."
Yes. There was no mistake. Peabody
grinned to himself. "And which way
was he headed?"

"Towards the mountains."

2

THE Reverend Brian Tyler stepped out on to the sidewalk. The sky was almost invisible beneath the curtain of steadily falling rain while the buildings across the way were hidden beneath the grey pall of clouds.

He couldn't help wondering, not for the first time, why God was making it so difficult for His servant to do what was, after all, His work. Tyler came to his usual conclusion: God was testing him. Well God needn't worry. Tyler wasn't going to fail or give up; not when he had come so far nor when he was so excited about the task in front of him.

But surely it wouldn't have hurt if the message had arrived in the summer when travel would have been so much easier and more pleasant; and he could have kept himself and his clothes dry.

Everyone had warned him that late winter wasn't the best season to travel, especially when it meant crossing the mountains. It would be best to wait until Spring was well under way. But the message had arrived before Christmas and come March he felt he'd waited long enough.

The people of Rock Springs wanted a preacher. And he wanted to take up the post, be part of a settled community, have his own church. It wasn't fair to deprive either them or himself any longer. He'd started out as soon as the snow disappeared from the valleys, although the wet slush and mud left behind hardly made ideal travelling conditions.

Tyler had been an itinerant preacher in California, riding from town to town, bringing the word of God to miners, cattlemen, whores and Indians. That sort of lifestyle — hard, dangerous and mostly uncomfortable — had been all right when he was younger. It was not so good now that he was in his early thirties.

So when he'd seen the advertisement, placed in a San Francisco newspaper by a small community in the Colorado Rockies, asking for a preacher, he'd immediately applied. Not just because it promised an easier way of life but more importantly because he felt it would be good to be among people who desired, rather than merely tolerated, or even were hostile to, his presence. Some correspondence had followed before he was formally offered the position.

Money had come from Rock Springs for the journey. Enough not only to buy supplies and a horse, but also to hire a guide.

Tyler didn't bother with the latter. He'd always had to be careful before spending money, and being quite able to look after himself and find his own way around the country, he set off all alone.

And ended up here in a small town on the edge of the mountains where he acknowledged that from now on he needed a guide. He wasn't so foolish as to rely on himself, or on God, to get him through the Rockies.

That had been a week ago. He'd spent the time since then, drumming his heels in what passed for a hotel, listening to the old-timers who had nothing better to do than gossip, waiting for the weather to improve.

Now, although it was still raining, several of the old-timers told him it would soon stop and that some of the muleskinners would be heading for the mountains in the next day or two.

Pulling his hat further down on his head and pulling the collar of his slicker up round his neck, Tyler hurried along the sidewalk to the stock pens at the far end of town. It was here that the mules and oxen were kept and he was pleased to see that several men were moving about amongst the animals, getting them ready for the next stage of their journeys.

Clinging mud oozed at his boots as

he trudged across the corral to where three men pushed five mules over to the fence. Tyler closed his ears to their cursing. He knew that mules only obeyed men who cursed profanely and who took the Lord's name very much in vain.

"Mr Jackson?" he asked as he approached them. "Wilbur Jackson?"

The three men stopped what they were doing and turned to look at him.

"Yeah, I'm Jackson," the eldest said.

They all looked much the same; the youngest at about twenty, being some ten years younger than the other two. They were ugly with large noses and piggy eyes, dressed in shabby clothes and down-at-heel boots.

"I'm the Reverend Brian Tyler."

"A preacherman?"

"Yes, that's right." Tyler revealed his clerical collar. "Some men at the hotel said you were going into the mountains towards Denver."

"Yeah, tomorrow."

19

"I wonder if you'd let me travel with you. At least most of the way. I'm heading for a place called Rock Springs."

"What the hell you going there for?" the second brother asked. "Ain't much in Rock Springs, not now the mine is played out."

"I've been asked to establish a church there."

"A church, eh?" Wilbur said. "That's a mighty fine thing."

"Can you help me? I could pay you out of the funds that the good people have collected to build the church."

"They've sent you money?"

"Not all of it. Just enough to help me with my travelling expenses. However, I've been careful and I still have most of it with me." Tyler patted his coat's inside pocket. "It'll help towards buying things like prayer books and Bibles."

"We'd be mighty proud to do what we can." Wilbur stepped forward to take Tyler's hand and shake it heartily. "We're always ready to help. Mr Tyler, these are my brothers, Otis and young Elmer."

More handshakes followed.

"Why mebbe we could even take you right into Rock Springs. What d'you say, Otis?"

"Yeah, why not?"

"I wouldn't want to take you out of your way."

"Wouldn't be no trouble. 'Sides it's up to everyone to help those who want to bring religion to these parts."

"The sinners sure need it!" Elmer muttered.

"It's very kind of you. How long do you think the journey will take?"

"Quite a while," Wilbur replied. "Depends on the weather too. Although it looks like you're gonna be lucky. Perhaps God is smiling on you." He gave Tyler one of his own blackened toothed smiles.

"I hope so."

"We'll be leaving first thing in the morning, so long as it ain't raining too hard. Real early. Can you be ready?"

21

Tyler nodded firmly.

"Good. We'll see you then."

Tyler walked back to the hotel with a light spring in his step. He would be on his way at last. He had to admit that on first seeing the three Jackson brothers he'd had some misgivings about them; he should have known better. Looks were deceptive. Their roughhewn faces and their smell were just part of their rude way of life. Unfortunate but inevitable. Underneath they were kind and trustworthy. God might provide in mysterious ways — but there was no doubt about it, He always did provide.

3

WITH some of the money he'd stolen, Jarrod bought food — bread, bacon, tins of beans — from another farmer along the way. It wasn't much but he reckoned it would last him until he came to a town.

For the next couple of days he tried, as far as possible, to keep to the valleys. There the snow had almost gone, although ice still formed along by the riverbanks, and there was deep snow on the mountain peaks. He was glad of the thick clothes he'd stolen, especially at night, when it turned cold and the recent rain made it difficult to find anything dry enough to light a fire.

He was starting to allow himself to feel hopeful. Utah couldn't be that far away and once there he was sure he could find shelter amongst the Mormons. They had no particular reason to like the authorities and perhaps no wish to hand anyone over to them.

On the third night he camped in the ruins of an old hut, all that remained of what once belonged to an unsuccessful sheepherder. The next morning when he got up and went out to his horse, something struck the wall next to his cheek, followed closely by the sound of a rifle shot.

"Jesus!" Startled Jarrod stumbled backwards and fell over.

The action saved his life as more shots quickly followed, all striking close to where he'd been standing. From the ground he looked up. The shots came from an outcrop of rocks on the hill opposite. The bounty hunter? No, there was more than one rifle. A posse after him because he'd robbed that farmer? Whoever it was didn't really matter. Sooner or later they wouldn't miss.

Heart pounding, he scrambled

backwards towards the broken doorway and half crouched in it. These days he was always careful. He only unsaddled his horse when he was certain he was safe, and now the bags with the food in them were still secured to the saddlehorn. A quick glance into the hut revealed nothing that couldn't be left behind, except for his rifle. That he needed.

Keeping his head low he dashed over to it, quickly grabbing it up.

"You down there," a voice came from the rocks. "Give up. Come on out with your hands up." Silence for a moment or two, then. "Or we'll start shooting again."

Jarrod wasn't sure about this chance to surrender. They'd been a bit too willing to shoot first, and only thought about letting him give up after. And what if they didn't shoot him out of hand and he did surrender? He'd end up in prison; or perhaps dangling at the end of a rope.

"Wait, wait," he called back in the

hope of fooling them, at least for the moment he'd need to get to his horse.

"Come out, now!"

Jarrod flung himself out of the hut. Immediately the firing began again. He fumbled for his horse's reins, got them free and went to throw himself up in the saddle. The horse was jittery, backing away from him, and he stumbled. Before he could recover, someone grabbed hold of his coat, pulling him backwards. Off balance he slipped and before he could do anything found himself being thrown to the ground out of sight of those firing at him.

Crying out in fright, Jarrod landed on his back. He stared up into the face of the bounty hunter.

The man grinned. "I'm not about to let some penny-ante posse get you for stealing from a farmer when I've got you for robbing stagecoaches. You're coming with me."

"Damn that," Jarrod muttered.

Coming up in a spring, he hefted the rifle he still carried.

The man tried to dodge but was taken by surprise and the barrel caught him in the chest. He went down and, breathing heavily, ignoring the sudden pains in his leg, Jarrod ran as fast as he could back to his horse. Behind him the bounty hunter pulled a pistol from his pocket and fired. The bullet whined past Jarrod's ear.

Before he could fire again, Jarrod had reached his horse. This time he managed to get into the saddle

The men from the posse were approaching the hut. Jarrod sent several shots towards them in the hope of stopping them.

Then kicking his heels into the horse's sides he urged it up the hill.

Bullets followed him but whether they were from the posse or the bounty hunter he didn't know. He didn't look back to find out.

He hadn't realized the bounty hunter was so close to catching him. Utah and its flat deserts, where pursuit would be easy, would have to wait. Instead he'd have to head further into the reaches of the Rockies, where hopefully he could lose all those people who were chasing him.

4

"**W**ELL, this is good news." Marshal Cox put down the piece of paper the traveller had brought in.

"What is it, Marshal?" Gus Wilkinson turned from the window where he was looking out at the street's few activities.

"Mr Tyler, the preacher, is on his way." Cox looked at the date of the letter — five weeks ago. The delivery of post to a remote spot like Rock Springs was always a matter of chance, especially in the winter, depending as it did on those crossing the Rockies agreeing to make a detour. So long as the weather, and the Indians, had been on his side, Tyler could be in town any day.

Cox stood up. "There'll be a lot to do, Gus."

"Yeah, OK. What shall I do?" Gus spoke eagerly, anxious to prove himself as the man's Deputy, a position to which he had only recently been appointed. He was just turned twenty and had a lanky look as if he still suffered from not knowing how to deal with his arms and legs. His hair was long and fair and in order to look older he was growing a moustache, which mostly consisted of a few sprouting whiskers.

Some members of the Town Council had said that a town the size of Rock Springs didn't need two full time lawmen. Cox had argued that he wasn't getting any younger — he was now in his late forties — and that, if the arrival of the preacher attracted more people to the area, he would need help. The Town Council had relented when Cox had also pointed out that, as Gus was young and inexperienced, he wouldn't need to be paid much.

Gus wasn't meant to know that but he suspected something of the sort. To try to make up for his immaturity he always wore his badge where everyone could see it, and swaggered around town, carrying two guns tied down in fancy holsters, although so far he hadn't had to use them.

Rock Springs was quiet now. That didn't mean it would always remain so. And Cox hoped that nothing ever happened that would force the young man to grow up too quickly.

"Perhaps you can go and see Mrs Goodman, make sure she's got his room ready at the boarding house. Mr Hobson will also have to be told so he can finish his plans. You can do that too. I'll let my wife know. She'll want to start preparing for the welcoming party she's going to give Mr Tyler."

★ ★ ★

Naomi Cox examined the sheet sewn inexpertly together from various pieces of cloth. She glanced at the anxious eyes of her younger companion and

31

knew she couldn't be critical. She felt sorry for Ginny Howland, who was having to manage on the small amount of money her husband earned from odd jobs around town, and which he didn't then gamble away.

Ginny was a young woman, good looking, and should have been settled in her own home, thinking of starting a family.

Instead she was here in Rock Springs, living in a room at the boarding house, ekeing out an existence with someone whom Naomi considered of not much account; although Ginny appeared to love Parker well enough.

"Is it all right?"

"Yes, dear, very nice." Naomi put the sheet to one side. Her husband could use it down at the jail. "Here," she picked up her purse and handed Ginny a few coins, "that's what we agreed, isn't it?"

"No, it's too much," Ginny protested. Her honesty was another thing Naomi liked about her. The girl glanced at the clock ticking on the mantelshelf over a roaring fire. "I'd better be going. Thanks for everything, Mrs Cox."

Naomi accompanied her to the door. "Thank goodness it's stopped raining. Perhaps Spring is on the way at last."

"I hope so."

"This was your first winter in the Rockies, wasn't it?"

Ginny nodded, pulling her shawl up over her head. "It used to rain in Georgia but never like it does here. It wasn't so cold either."

Gently, Naomi touched her arm. "Once the warm weather arrives you'll feel better. It's quite a pretty place in the summer. And Nigel has received a message that our new preacher has started on his way. He should be here any day."

"Oh, that's good."

"When Mr Tyler arrives and starts his services, Rock Springs will get away from the bawdy reputation it gained when it was a mining town. That should encourage families to settle here." Naomi kissed Ginny on the cheek and watched as she walked down to the gate and turned towards Main Street

Ginny was twenty-three, with light brown hair curling down to her shoulders, brown eyes and high cheekbones. As she walked she bent towards the wind, clutching her shawl tighter to her, wondering, not for the first time, exactly what she was doing here.

Back in Georgia, she had married her neighbour, Parker Howland, being very much in love with him. His family was wealthier than the Kilklines, his father owning a large, prosperous farm and numerous slaves. However, Parker had never had much interest in farming. He'd always wanted to find his fortune in the West.

Soon after their marriage, both Ginny's parents had died. Their few slaves fled, the farm was run down, and it seemed likely that her brother had been killed in the fighting. It was obvious that the South was going to lose the war. The Yankees were on their way. There was no reason to stay in Georgia.

So Ginny had gladly agreed to head for Colorado and the riches surely to be found there.

At first things went well. They'd arrived in Denver and hired a pretty little house out by Cripple Creek.

The trouble was that although Parker wanted to find fame and fortune, he had no idea of how to go about it. He had always fancied himself something of a gentleman, wearing good clothes and carrying a silver topped cane and he didn't want to indulge in anything he considered beneath a gentleman; such as work. One evening out drinking with some friends he got into an idle poker game and won a considerable amount of money.

That, and the fact that gambling was considered a gentleman's sport, had made up his mind. He would become a gambler.

Unfortunately, that first good win had seldom been repeated. Parker was honest enough that he refused to cheat; unlike most of those he played against, so while he won at times, he lost more often.

It meant that within a space of a couple of months they had had to leave the pretty little house in Denver behind and move to something smaller and not so pretty. More moves had quickly followed until they were now here, in Rock Springs, living in one room at Mrs Goodman's.

As she picked her way through the cloying mud, Ginny sighed.

Parker still gambled. Because, here, the other players weren't up to much, he mostly won. But now he was gambling with people who had as little money as he did. So his winnings never amounted to a great deal. Reluctantly he sometimes did a few odd jobs around town but Ginny had to rely more and more on the kindness of such as Naomi Cox and Mrs Goodman to provide her with the means of earning a few extra dollars.

Ginny still loved Parker but she wasn't sure how much longer she could go on living like this.

★ ★ ★

Parker Howland was beginning to feel much the same way.

He'd sat all morning playing poker with a couple of miners travelling through to Denver.

The saloon had once thrived as one of the many meeting places of Rock Springs' inhabitants. Now it employed only one prostitute and it was difficult to find more than one table of card players, except maybe on a Saturday night.

Howland was the closest thing to a gambler left in the town and he knew he wasn't about to make a living out of it.

The trouble was he didn't know what else to do. Ginny wouldn't take too kindly to yet another move. Anyway to move would only mean going somewhere else just like Rock Springs.

Ginny would be on at him to help build the church once the preacher arrived. Howland had no real excuse not to do so. Back on his father's farm he'd had to turn his hand to many things and that included carpentry. But to play cards he depended on his hands and he didn't want them blistered or scratched, although he doubted if Ginny would think that an acceptable excuse.

Still today, he'd taken the miners for almost all they had; which came to a few cents over five dollars. Not exactly a fortune. In fact it was only enough to pay Mrs Goodman at the boarding house for another week, and perhaps treat Ginny to a meal at the cafe.

Thinking of Ginny, he looked at his watch. It was noon already. He'd promised to meet her and help with the shopping.

She'd be waiting.

"That's me finished," he said, sitting back in the chair and stretching.

"Aw, come on, how about a chance to get even?"

Howland shook his head. "Sorry, I've got to go." He scooped up his winnings. "See you, gents." And he went out of the smoky, ill-lit saloon into the street.

★ ★ ★

Walking quickly down Main Street to the general store, Ginny saw him and felt a spurt of annoyance. Parker had promised that he wouldn't gamble for long and here he was just coming out of the saloon.

Then he saw her and smiled. She forgot everything except how fine he looked and how she'd always loved him. He was twenty-seven not much taller than she was, but oh so handsome with his dark curly hair, dark moustache and dark brooding eyes.

He broke into a quick walk heading towards her and much to the amusement of the few passersby, took her into his arms, swinging her round.

"I won! More than five dollars!" He made it sound like a fortune. "Come on, Ginny, let's go celebrate. I'll treat you to a slap up lunch at the cafe."

'Slap up' was a bit of an exaggeration for any meal served at the town's small cafe but Ginny suddenly felt too light hearted to quibble. Spring was coming, the preacher was due at any minute and Parker had won. Things could only improve.

"All right," she said.

And arm in arm they walked down the sidewalk.

5

AFTER a few days travel, the weather took a distinct turn for the better. A smell of new life was in the air and the breeze felt almost warm, while here and there were glimpses of the year's first flowers. Not that it made the going any easier, as the mule train followed a narrow trail leading sharply down through closely packed pine trees. The sure-footed mules didn't falter but once or twice Tyler wondered if they would fall over the edge.

He was getting impatient, although he tried not to show it. It would do no good and might upset his guides. It wasn't the Jacksons' fault they were making such slow progress. He told himself that the difficulty of the journey was yet another of God's tests. But he wished the mule train would go

41

a little faster. And wished too that the mountain pass towards which they were headed didn't always look as far away in the evening as it had in the morning.

"We'd better stop here for the night." Wilbur came to a halt holding up his arm as a signal to his brothers to stop the mules.

They had emerged from the trees onto a stretch of open ground halfway down the mountainside. In front of them the trees closed in again, promising more difficult going.

"Don't look so disappointed, preacher, I know there's still a couple of hours of daylight left but this is a good spot to make camp. We might not find another and it'll be dark and maybe dangerous before we reach the bottom of the slope."

Wilbur was clearly right.

Tyler got off his horse, stretching wearily. The other three were experienced mule-skinners, quick and efficient at loading and unloading the packs and at setting up a reasonably neat campsite. Usually Tyler limited himself to seeing to his own animal and helping gather wood for the fire.

Tonight he noticed nothing unusual until he turned round from unsaddling his horse.

The Jackson brothers were standing nearby staring at him. They hadn't bothered to start a fire or unload the mules. Something was clearly wrong because, while they might be slovenly in their own dress and cleanliness, they were good at seeing to the animals on whom they depended for their livelihood.

Elmer was smiling but Wilbur and Otis looked hard and serious.

"What's the matter?"

"Hand it over," Wilbur said.

"Hand what over?"

"Your money, preacher, what else?"

"And while you're at it you can give us your fancy duds!" Elmer added, a greedy gleam in his eyes. "I reckon your boots will fit me fine."

"Wait a minute," Tyler began angrily. "I employed you in good faith . . ."

Wilbur smiled. "Unfortunately we ain't very interested in faith, not your kind anyhow."

"No," Otis hawked and spat. "All this talk about church and religion don't mean nothing to us. We want your money."

"I said I would pay you."

"We want it *all*."

Tyler was angry. He was also frightened. He'd trusted these men and their object all along had been to bring him out here into the wilderness and rob him. Perhaps worse. He'd been in enough precarious situations amongst rough men to know that reasoning or pleading would do no good.

There were three of them; the odds weren't exactly good. But Tyler wasn't about to give up the hard saved money of the good people of Rock Springs without a fight.

He shoved his coat back, reaching for the gun he kept in a hidden holster at the back of his belt.

The Jacksons stared at him, unmoving, as if unable to take in the fact that a man of God was willing to resort to violence. Tyler didn't like it either. Shooting another human being was hard to justify. But there were times on the violent frontier when violence was the only thing that violent people understood. It wasn't the first time he'd been in a situation where to do nothing would have meant his own death rather than that of his assailant.

Then Wilbur yelled. "Get him!" And it was too late.

Otis and Elmer charged him. Tyler got off one shot, that missed, before Otis grabbed his gun arm while Elmer caught him round the waist. The gun went off again, harmlessly into the air this time. Somehow Otis forced it out of his hand and threw it away. Tyler, who had been known to indulge in fisticuffs, got in one or two hard punches, causing his opponents to grunt in pain. Elmer went down on one knee out of the fight for a moment but, before Tyler could take advantage of it, Wilbur moved forward to join in.

He and Otis grappled Tyler to the ground in a blur of arms and legs, punches and kicks. Helpless he lay there, curled up in a ball, pain shooting up and down his spine.

"Stupid sonofabitch," Wilbur said and put his boot hard into Tyler's ribs. "Get his damn money."

"No," Tyler mumbled between cut lips.

Hands grabbed at his coat pulling it off him. Otis and Elmer fought over it until Otis cried out in triumph. "Here it is!" He threw the purse in which Tyler had carefully hoarded the money towards Wilbur, who caught it deftly.

"Let's take the rest of his clothes!" Elmer said.

Tyler had rarely felt so scared in his life. He was all alone. No one was about to rescue him. The Jacksons would not stop at stealing his clothes.

He could identify them. They'd have a bit more fun with him and then they'd shoot him. Tyler didn't want to die here in the mountains with no one knowing.

He tried to get to his feet, slipped, was kicked in the backside and fell again. He scrambled to his knees, slipped again on the muddy ground and another vicious kick sent him sprawling over the edge of the clearing.

Into nothing.

He screamed, his hands scrabbling uselessly at the rocks. With a sickening lurch of his stomach he saw the tops of the trees in the valley far far below spinning up towards him. His scream was abruptly cut off as he hit a narrow rocky ledge, several feet below the cliff-edge. He bounced painfully and, before he could roll off, clutched desperately at the root of a mesquite bush growing there. He wriggled further onto the ledge, lying on its rocky safety, panting for breath.

"Where the hell's he gone?" Wilbur

demanded from a long way above him.

Tyler pulled his bruised body closer into the cliff-face. Glancing up he saw the shadows of the Jacksons as they peered over the edge but he couldn't actually see them and he prayed they wouldn't see him either.

"He didn't fall all that way did he?" That was Otis. "I don't think he did. We'd have heard him wouldn't we?"

"He musta done. He ain't there. Hell! Hold on. There's a ledge."

Tyler felt his heart almost stop beating.

"Can't see nothing."

"Well it don't matter much if the bastard is down there or iffen he ain't," Wilbur decided. "He won't be able to get back up and no one ain't likely to come by 'cept maybe a few Indians or a wild bear or two." He chuckled at the preacher's likely fate.

"What about his clothes?" Elmer whined.

"Damn his clothes, boy! We ain't got time to worry about them. We've got his money now. You can buy any amount of clothes you want with that. Don't know what you want new clothes for anyhow."

"Come on, kid," Otis added before Wilbur lost his temper.

Elmer paused for a moment looking down towards the ledge. "Pity about them there boots though. I surely did like them boots."

Then they were gone. Not very long after Tyler heard the mules moving out; a few curses from the Jacksons came down to him on the wind. Followed by silence.

He breathed a sigh of relief. A relief quickly replaced by despair. For even as he felt unconsciousness creeping towards him he knew he wasn't safe. Wilbur Jackson was right. He was stuck here on a narrow ledge with no means of getting back to the top of the cliff. And he surely couldn't go down. No help was likely.

6

THE fire was burning well — not so brightly that it would tell any pursuers where Jarrod was, but well enough to give off warmth and comfort. And cooking over it was a rabbit that he had shot that afternoon. It was still too early in the year for there to be much game around and the rabbit was a scrawny thing, but he considered it a good omen.

He felt safe — there had been no more sign of the posse or the bounty hunter. He'd outrun them. The next day when he reached the valley he could head for Utah.

The rabbit was cooked and he was just going to enjoy his first bite when he heard a groan.

Jarrod peered round. He could see no one and nothing. He must have been mistaken. It was the wind.

51

"Help me." The voice was indistinct, the words almost impossible to make out. But this time Jarrod knew he wasn't hearing things.

Suspecting some sort of trick, he jumped to his feet, hand snatching at his gun. A bit dismayed at how ready to shoot he was, he stalked the clearing.

"Who's there?" he called and from somewhere beyond the cliff came another groan. Carefully he approached the edge and getting down on his hands and knees looked over it. In the dark of the early night he just about made out a rocky ledge some way below. And lying on it was a bundle of clothes and the white oblong of a face staring up at him.

"Help me." The plea came again.

"Wait there."

"I haven't got anywhere else to go, son."

Jarrod struggled up and hurried over to his horse. He picked up the rope, tied one end round the saddlehorn and led the animal to the cliff edge. He threw the rope's other end down to whoever was lying there.

"Are you hurt?"

"Yes. Quite badly."

"Damn." Jarrod swore under his breath. "Can you climb up on your own? Because I don't know how the hell I'm going to get you to the top otherwise."

"I don't know about hell but God might help." The voice chuckled leaving Jarrod puzzled wondering what the man was talking about.

He stared down. "Tie the rope securely round your waist."

"It's done."

"All right, boy." Jarrod patted the horse's nose. Slowly he inched the animal backwards. "Careful, take it easy. You OK, sir?"

A grunt came in reply.

Before long hands appeared clutching at the rocks. Jarrod stopped the horse and went over to the man, putting his arms round him, hauling him up into the clearing.

The man said something that sounded like 'Thank God' and fainted.

Jarrod wondered who he was and what he was doing on the ledge. He'd been beaten up, that much was obvious. By the light of the campfire he could see bruises standing out blackly on the man's face. He wasn't wearing a coat and his hands and mouth had already turned blue with cold. Quickly Jarrod dragged him closer to the fire, wrapping him up in the stolen slicker. That was all he could do for him. Whether the man lived or died was up to him and the God he'd mentioned.

Jarrod went back to his rabbit.

★ ★ ★

Some way away the Jackson brothers lazed around their own campfire. Wilbur had opened the preacher's purse, emptied the money on the ground, and was painstakingly counting it.

Otis licked his lips. "How much we get?"

"Almost twenty dollars."

Elmer whistled through the gap in his teeth. Twenty dollars! That sounded like an awful lot of money and he began to imagine all he could buy with it. Girls and drink were foremost on the list but new clothes, especially fancy boots, weren't far behind.

Otis nudged his younger brother and grinned.

Wilbur sighed. Sometimes it was difficult being the brother of two idiots who both believed twenty dollars was a fortune.

Still meeting the preacher and stealing his money had been a lucky break. The twenty dollars was money they hadn't earned after all. Perhaps this year they'd actually sell their goods for a profit. If the preacher believed in miracles then so could Wilbur.

★ ★ ★

It was morning before the man woke up. He blinked blearily across at Jarrod sitting on the other side of the embers of a fire.

"How you feeling?"

"All right, I think." Tyler put a hand to his head. "Is there any coffee?" he added, looking hopefully at the battered pot.

"Yeah. I've only got one mug though. Wait a minute." Jarrod emptied it of the dregs of his drink, poured out a fresh mugful and handed it across. "Who are you? What are you doing way out here?"

It was a good question. Tyler wasn't quite sure. The last thing he remembered was falling through the air towards his death. Obviously he hadn't died because this young man looked like neither an angel nor a devil. Somehow he collected his jumbled thoughts together; and wasn't very pleased once he had.

"My name's Brian Tyler. I'm a preacher. And some goddamned men

I trusted to take me to my new church turned round and robbed me. I'm not sure whether I'm angrier at them or at myself. What a damn fool they must have taken me for! And what a damn fool I was!"

Jarrod gaped at him. Tyler might be a preacher but he wasn't a bit like Parson Bateman back home in Georgia. He would never have sworn, lost his temper or travelled into the wilderness on his own.

"They beat you and robbed you?"

"And left me to die! Goddammit! I suppose," Tyler looked round the clearing, "they took my horse too?"

"There wasn't a sign of one when I got here."

"Dammit! Now I've got no money, no coat and no horse! By the way," Tyler looked a bit shamefaced, "I haven't thanked you for saving my life. Nor do I know your name."

Jarrod paused slightly before saying, "It's Jarrod Kilkline." Quickly he handed Tyler the coffeepot and hoping to change the subject from himself, went on, "Do you feel up to eating some rabbit? There's some left from last night."

After a while Jarrod got to his feet and began packing up his few things. "What are you going to do now?" He expected that the preacher would want his help in getting to the nearest town where he could report the robbery and seek help.

Instead he surprised Jarrod by saying, "Go on to Rock Springs of course. People are waiting for me there."

"How? You said yourself you haven't got a horse or any money."

"God will provide."

"It doesn't seem like He's done that much for you up till now."

"He saved me from dying by sending you."

Jarrod sighed. The lot of Good Samaritan sat heavily on his shoulders. "Where is this place you're heading for?"

"It's over near Denver. It shouldn't

be too far. I guess it'll take me a while to walk it but I'll get there in the end."

Jarrod realized Tyler was serious. "All right," he sighed again in defeat. "I'll help you get there."

He had the feeling he was going to regret this. Yet what else could he do? He couldn't leave a fellow traveller, a man of God, out here, alone, because if he did Tyler would probably die.

Besides if anyone was still on his trail they would be looking for someone on his own. They wouldn't be looking for two men riding together, one of whom was a preacher. And Rock Springs was probably as good a place as any other to hide out in for a while.

"Were you going to Denver?"

"No, Utah."

"You're going the wrong way."

"I know."

Again Tyler noticed the pause and the fact that Jarrod didn't elaborate on what he said. He had the feeling he'd landed up with another thief — the difference being that this one hadn't tried to rob *him*.

"If you go to Rock Springs you'll be going even further out of your way."

"It doesn't matter."

"I can't pay you."

"That doesn't matter either. You want help and I'm willing to give it. Don't argue. Are you ready to go?"

Tyler stood up, wincing and groaning at the ache in his ribs which he hoped weren't broken. "Why are you doing this, really?"

Jarrod couldn't very well tell him the truth.

"You said it yourself, Mr Tyler. God will provide. And right now He's provided me."

7

THE group of buildings was almost hidden beyond the curve of the hill, pine trees clustering all round. The place could hardly justify being called a town. It consisted of a general store, a saloon, a livery stable with a freight yard at the back, and a couple of squalid huts, all grouped about a muddy square.

It was late afternoon when it came into view, misty rain obscuring visibility. And it was cold. But however small and wretched, to both Jarrod and Tyler it looked a welcoming spot to stop for the night.

"And I can buy a few things," Tyler said. "Especially a coat and a gun."

"A gun?" Jarrod asked in some surprise.

"Yes, those bastards took mine. I know it's not very preacher like to carry a gun but there are times when it's necessary." From his tone it was obvious Tyler didn't mean he wanted one for shooting game.

"How are you going to pay? I thought those men took your money."

Tyler smiled. "Not quite *all* of it. I had a few dollars hidden in my right boot. Luckily Elmer didn't get to steal my clothes."

"You surely know all about survival in the wilderness."

"You got that right."

At the livery stable Tyler spent a few minutes dickering with the stable owner. In the end he managed to buy a played out old nag which was all he could afford.

"She'll get you where you're going so long as you don't want to get there fast," the man said with a toothless grin.

They next went to the general store where Tyler bought a thick jacket, a revolver and bullets, while Jarrod spent some of his stolen money on food.

"Anywhere here we can stay the night?" he asked the man who served them.

"I've got a room out back. Best if you sleep there. The saloon can get a bit rough. And I don't charge so much. I can throw in breakfast as well."

"Thanks," Tyler said. He then surprised Jarrod all over again by agreeing to go over to the saloon with him and offering to buy them both whiskey.

The store owner was right. The saloon wasn't much of a place. An ill-fitting door led into one long low ceilinged room, with rough planks for walls and floor, the latter covered with unswept sawdust. Several oil lamps hung from the ceiling, their smoke adding to the general murk. The bar was nothing more than a piece of wood resting on old barrels, at one end of which an opening led to a steep flight of stairs. A few tables and stools stood in the middle of the floor.

There weren't many customers. Some

old-timers, several miners and a couple of young men who looked like out of work cowboys. Two women wandered amongst them while a grizzled man with a long grey beard served the drinks. They all stopped to stare at the newcomers but sensing they weren't going to cause any trouble soon went back to whatever it was they were doing.

"Here's to you, Jarrod," Tyler said, downing his whiskey in one go.

Jarrod followed suit. And wished he hadn't. The whiskey was obviously the bartender's own particular brand of snakejuice. It made his eyes water while he gasped for breath.

"Perhaps we'd better stick to beer," Tyler grinned, banging Jarrod on the back. Then he turned serious. "I never really thanked you, not properly, for what you did back there. I wish I could do something for you in return."

Jarrod doubted whether anyone could do anything for him and he said, a bit suspiciously, "Such as?"

"Well it's obvious that something is troubling you . . . "

"I'm all right. There's nothing wrong."

"Don't lie, Jarrod. You could confide in me."

Jarrod was suddenly tempted. Even if this man couldn't help him it would be nice to unburden himself to a sympathetic ear. Then one of the miners came up to the bar and jostled him to one side, shouting out for service. The moment was lost.

As the evening wore on some of the men started up a couple of poker games.

"I think I'll go play," Jarrod said, hoping that maybe he'd win enough to pay for an hour or so with one of the whores; although naturally he didn't say so to the preacher. Tyler was broad minded about most things but he probably wouldn't approve of that.

"I'll see you back at the store, then." Tyler watched the young man take his beer and join a group of miners.

He idled round the saloon, nodding and smiling at those who looked at him, wondering if any of these poor sinners would appreciate an open-air service in the morning. Even the most hardened frontiersman sometimes liked to be reminded of God, home and his mother.

He had just reached the stairs by the bar when he saw a young girl coming down them. She was quite pretty with long dark brown hair hanging in waves halfway down her back, and dark eyes. She was much younger than the other two women but was dressed in similar fashion with a low cut dress, showing off the rise of her slight bosom, leaving Tyler in no doubt that she too was a prostitute. And although she was only about fifteen her hard life was already beginning to take its toll on her features.

He was appalled. He knew and accepted that men wanted women, and that out here, in the West, women, especially good ones, were in a minority. Prostitutes were necessary and provided lonely men with perhaps the only female companionship they were likely to know. It didn't mean he approved, especially when some girls were forced, through varying circumstances, into the life. He was quite sure that any girl, here in this rough saloon amongst these rough men, would soon become hurt and degraded. And she was so young.

Seeing him watching her, the girl put on a professional smile. "Hi there, honey, can I do anything for you?"

"Yes, I think you can."

"Pay the bartender." She tried not to sound as tired as she obviously felt.

Tyler put some coins down on the bar, the tender nodded and he took the girl's arm, supporting her as they climbed the stairs.

Jarrod watched them go, feeling disappointed in his companion.

★ ★ ★

The girl's bedroom was tiny and dirty, the only pieces of furniture the bed, a rickety table and a chair with the stuffing coming out of it. Her few clothes hung on hooks behind the door. It was cold — there was little heating, just a slight warmth coming from the stove in the corner, no rugs on the warped floor and only a few moth-eaten blankets on the bed.

Once inside, the girl put her arms round Tyler's neck and kissed him expertly.

"No child," he said gently and removed her arms, putting her from him.

She looked scared. "What do you want then?"

"What's your name?"

"Myra."

"Myra?"

"Yeah, just Myra. Now, mister, what is it you want? There are other customers you know."

"There's no need to bother about them. I've paid enough for your time.

Sit down. I just want to talk to you."

Myra sat down on the bed and Tyler sat beside her, taking one of her hands in his.

"I'm a preacher. My name's Brian Tyler and I'd like to help you."

Tears came into the girl's eyes. "No one can help me, mister. I'm a whore and have been since I was thirteen. It's too late. I'll always be a whore."

"It's never too late to change, Myra. Never too late to seek God's help. Tell me, how did a child like you come to be here in this place?"

"My parents were killed in an accident when I was ten and my Uncle and Aunt took me in. Soon after their farm failed and they decided to travel to California. On the way my Aunt took sick and died. My Uncle decided he wanted more money than he had and he . . . he sold my body along the way to whoever could pay. I tried to make him stop but he just beat me till I agreed."

Myra put her face in her hands

and sobbed bitterly while Tyler held her gently and waited until she could go on.

"I hated him and what he made me do. I intended to escape from him once we got to California, where surely we would have stopped in a decent town and I could have told someone my sad story. By the time we got here it was almost winter and the weather got so bad we had to stay. My Uncle spent his time gambling and when it came time for us to leave, he'd lost everything and couldn't pay his debts. The bartender, Mr Rogers, said he'd take me instead."

Tyler gave an exclamation of disgust.

"I begged and pleaded my Uncle not to leave me. But he needed the money more'n he needed me. That was two years ago. I've been here ever since."

"Can't you leave?" Tyler knew it was a stupid question even as he asked it, and wasn't surprised at Myra's scornful reply.

"Of course not. Mr Rogers takes any

money I earn and the other whores keep an eye on me. 'Sides where would I go? This, mister, in case you hadn't noticed, is in the middle of nowhere."

"I'm sure there must be a way out of your predicament. We'd better pray for guidance."

But Tyler and Myra had no sooner got to their knees than a voice boomed out from downstairs.

"Myra! Myra! Where are you?"

"Oh no, it's Ronnie."

"Who's Ronnie?"

"Ronnie Bennett. He's a miner. He thinks he wants to marry me and he's ever so jealous."

"We're not doing anything for him to be jealous of . . . " Tyler got no further as the door banged open. He and Myra looked up.

A man in his thirties stood in the doorway, glaring. He had brown hair hanging to his shoulders, a brown beard halfway to his waist and he was incredibly large.

Myra screamed. "Ronnie, wait!"

71

Bennett took no notice. With an angry roar he grabbed hold of Tyler, hauling him to his feet, yelling. "What the hell are you doing with my girl?"

"I wasn't . . . "

Bennett wasn't interested in any explanation. He punched Tyler hard in the stomach and shoved him away, sending him flying through the doorway to land with a crash against the far wall. He slithered down it.

"Stop it!" Myra cried.

She ran up to Bennett but he pushed her away as well so she sprawled on the floor, while he stalked out into the hall. "Myra's my girl!" he yelled and picked up Tyler in order to fling him down again.

Below in the saloon all activity came to a halt as the customers listened to the fight.

"What's going on?" Jarrod asked his nearest neighbour.

"Ronnie Bennett's back in town. He's caught someone with Myra, when he wants her for himself. All hell will break loose now." The miner sounded pleased.

"Is Myra a young girl?"

"Yeah."

"Oh shit," Jarrod muttered. That was Tyler up there getting pummelled. Throwing down his cards and pausing only to scoop up his winnings, he got to his feet and hurried upstairs, reaching the top just as Bennett was about to stomp the preacher. A scared Myra crouched in the doorway. Jarrod realized talk would mean nothing to someone like Bennett. Instead he flung himself at the burly miner and they went down in a jumble of arms and legs.

Bennett seemed quite pleased at having a new adversary. With a roar of delight he shoved Jarrod off of him, kicked Tyler again and, dragging Jarrod up, caught hold of him in a bearhug. For a few moments they struggled together, Jarrod trying to free himself of the hold, Bennett determined to cling on. Then Bennett took a step backwards and missed his footing. Still holding on to one another he and Jarrod rolled down the stairs to land in a heap at the bottom.

Somehow Tyler got to his feet. Hearing the sounds of excited yells from below he stumbled down to the bar. Most of the men had gathered round Bennett and Jarrod, shouting encouragement to them to get up. Several, obviously friends of the miner's, showed an inclination to fight Tyler.

Quickly the preacher drew his gun and with a somewhat shaky hand, pointed it at them. "Back! Stand back!"

At the same time, Bennett got up, pulling Jarrod with him. Tyler acted before the miner could do any more damage. Stepping forward, he brought the gunbutt down hard on Bennett's head. With a groan the man collapsed.

Keeping an eye on Bennett's friends, Tyler reached out a hand helping Jarrod. Staggering they made it up the stairs, to where Myra waited.

"This way," she said and hurried down the hall to the far end. She opened a door onto an outside staircase. "Go on, quickly."

"What about you?" Tyler asked.

"Don't worry about me. You must leave. Ronnie will be madder'n hell. Go on." She gave the hesitant Tyler a push. "Please. I'll be all right."

Tyler didn't want to leave the girl but he didn't see what else he could do. He couldn't very well make her go with him and to delay arguing with her would mean Bennett and his friends catching him and Jarrod. He didn't think they'd survive the experience.

"Come on," Jarrod urged, clearly thinking much the same.

Once they were through the door, Myra shut and locked it.

"Let's hope that new horse of your's goes faster than the stable owner thought," Jarrod said as they ran towards the livery. "What the hell were you and that girl doing to make

75

Bennett so mad?"

"We were praying for guidance," Tyler said haughtily.

"Hmmm. I've never heard it called that before!"

8

JARROD eased himself in the saddle and stared along their backtrail. "It don't look like anyone is following us."

But it was difficult to really see because, although it was now morning, it was so cloudy and rainy it was difficult to tell when night ended and day began. He and Tyler had ridden for hours, scared that Ronnie Bennett and his friends would come after them, but it now seemed they hadn't done so.

"Thank God for that." Tyler dismounted and stretched wearily. The horse he'd bought wasn't only old and slow she was also bony and uncomfortable. "You know, Jarrod, I feel real bad about leaving poor Myra behind."

"So do I. But it was her choice

and if we'd stayed we'd only have been beaten up, perhaps even killed. We still couldn't have done anything for her."

"That doesn't make it any easier. God knows what that brute will do to her. It was all my fault. I should have made her come with us."

"It wouldn't have looked good if you'd arrived in Rock Springs with a whore on your arm." Jarrod raised a hand against Tyler's protestations. "I know you weren't doing anything wrong with her but until people get to know you, they might not be so ready to believe that. Anyway there's nothing you can do for her now. Maybe later you can go back and see if she's still there."

"Yes," Tyler sighed.

"Come on, Mr Tyler, it can't be all that far now. You'll feel better when you get to Rock Springs."

★ ★ ★

Wilbur Jackson strode along the sidewalk, face and body set in lines of anger. Otis and Elmer kept up with him but wisely several paces behind. Wilbur wasn't very happy. It was the same every time they came to Denver. No matter how clever or cunning they tried to be, the Denver merchants were always one step ahead and they sold their mules and the goods for far less than they were worth. Why had he thought this year would be any different?

He'd already tried to drown his sorrows in drink. That hadn't worked. Now he was looking for something else.

He came to an abrupt halt outside Miss Betty's Emporium, causing the other two to almost bang into him.

"Hey, Wilbur," Otis said in some alarm. "We can't go in there!"

"Why not?" Wilbur growled.

Everyone, even out-of-towners like the Jackson brothers, knew that Miss Betty's Emporium was one of Denver's fanciest cathouses; it would therefore charge the fanciest prices. Otis screwed up his courage to tell his unpredictable brother so.

"Well, you don't have to come in with me. But I'm going in and having a good time."

"Oh hell," said Otis. He didn't see why his brother should be the only one to enjoy himself and it was also common knowledge that the girls in Miss Betty's knew how to give their clients a real good time. It had been weeks since any of them had had the pleasure of a woman's company and if Wilbur deserved a treat so did he and Elmer. Perhaps the girls wouldn't cost *that* much or perhaps they could recoup some of their losses in a card game.

Wilbur was already going through the door and suddenly excited, Otis said, "Come on Elmer," and followed him.

★ ★ ★

In the event, when they finally reached Rock Springs, Brian Tyler wasn't too sure that he did, in fact, feel better.

Although he hid it well, inside he admitted his disappointment at his first sight of the town. He hadn't known what to expect but had imagined something like the small but sunny and clean towns he passed through in California. Rock Springs was small all right but it wasn't all that clean and it certainly wasn't sunny, shrouded as it was in misty rain, the mountains and the pine trees pressing uncomfortably close.

And on one hill to the west, as an ever present reminder of its rowdy origins, were the mine workings; deserted and falling into ruin, a scar on the landscape.

Like many another mining town it had risen from a group of shanty huts to become a reasonably wealthy place, with some decent, large buildings; until the mine played out and the miners moved on.

Now there was just one long main street left, where those few people who refused to let the place die, had stores. A fairly large jail remained, along with a courthouse of stone. The rest of the buildings were made of wood. Short streets of houses, some in disrepair, wound off into the hills. Two saloons and a not very good brothel were all that remained of what had once been a thriving redlight district, if the other closed and shuttered buildings were anything to go by.

Still Tyler knew it was too late to change his mind. He was here now and would have to make the best of it.

Jarrod was also disappointed — to see the jail and the courthouse. He'd hoped that a mining town in the Rockies wouldn't have any law. He should have known better. The town was heading towards respectability and, besides religion, that meant keeping the law. His hope had to be that no one up here in the mountains would have heard of someone wanted for robbery way down in the deserts of Arizona.

"Come on, Jarrod, let's go and introduce ourselves to the Marshal," Tyler said and reluctantly Jarrod followed him. He didn't much like going into a Marshal's office; he might not come out again.

"Mr Tyler! It's good to see you at last!" Cox leapt to his feet, shaking Tyler heartily by the hand. "It seemed you'd never arrive."

"You've got Jarrod Kilkline here to thank for my safety."

"Why, what happened?"

"I foolishly employed some strangers as my guides. They robbed me and left me for dead in the mountains."

"My God, how dreadful! It seems you can't trust anyone these days. Oh, this is Gus Wilkinson, my Deputy. Gus, go and tell Mr Hobson that Mr Tyler has arrived."

"Yes, sir."

"Would you like to swear out a complaint against these robbers?"

"Yes, but later. Right now I'd like

to get freshened up, change my clothes. Get used to sitting on something that doesn't sway. I seem to have been travelling forever."

"Of course, of course. Mrs Goodman over at the boarding house has got a room for you. She runs a good, clean place, and her cooking is plain but plentiful. She also has a lot of rules about meal times and locking up hours that her guests disobey at their peril!"

"What about Jarrod?"

"I'm sure she can find something for Mr Kilkline as well. She's not very busy at the moment and she's cheap."

Jarrod felt a bit annoyed that the Marshal could so easily recognize that he couldn't afford very much, but relieved at the same time that the room was cheap. He had a few dollars left from the money he'd won at the poker game before being disturbed by Ronnie Bennett but it wasn't much and it wouldn't last long.

"Come on. Everyone will be so pleased you're here, Mr Tyler. Naomi, my wife, is going to give a party in your honour. She's been working hard preparing for it. You'll feel up to attending, won't you?"

"Of course I will," Tyler said, although he wasn't sure he did. But how could he let everyone down? He knew that, for a while, until his novelty wore off, he would be subjected to stares and remarks, which he would just have to put up with.

"Come on then." As they left the jailhouse and started down the street, Cox turned to Jarrod. "You're not from around here, are you?"

"No, I'm from Georgia." No point denying that, his accent gave him away, but Jarrod was instantly cautious, although there didn't seem to be anything other than natural curiosity behind the man's question.

"Were you in the war?"

"Yes, sir."

"Was that when you got that limp?"

"Yeah."

Cox took the hint that Jarrod didn't

want to speak about the war or about himself. He looked at Jarrod carefully. Cox might be living out his last years as a lawman in a sleepy, small town, but he was still astute enough to recognize someone who was wary of the law. He didn't want any unnecessary trouble. Mr Kilkline might bear watching.

Mrs Goodman was short and plump and good natured under her strict exterior. Although she made a few remarks about extra work and only one pair of hands, she found Jarrod a bedroom. It was at the back, overlooking the kitchen, up three flights of ever narrowing stairs. It was her cheapest and plainest, because she too knew someone without much money. But it was clean with a narrow but many blanketed bed, a table and chair and several hooks for his clothes. And the bathroom was only one floor below.

Jarrod had a bath (hot water extra but worth the cost) and washed and combed his tangled hair into some sort of neatness. He didn't really want to go to the party for Mr Tyler. He didn't like being the centre of attention, and while Mr Tyler would be the object of most curiosity, he would come in for his fair share of attention because he'd helped the preacher.

But not to go might be to draw even more attention to himself. He'd seen the Marshal looking at him. He didn't want to do anything to arouse anyone's suspicions.

9

"DO you think there'll be enough?" Naomi Cox asked.

Hands on hips, Ginny surveyed the table that seemed almost to groan beneath the weight of pies, pastries, cakes, fruit and various drinks. She smiled, "It's more than enough. You could feed half of Denver on this, not merely the cream of Rock Springs society!"

Naomi smiled back, aware that the girl was right. "It's not often I get the chance to bake for a party. I wanted to make the most of it."

"I'm sure Mr Tyler will be impressed."

"I can't wait to meet him. Nigel says he's not much like a preacher. And there's that mysterious companion of his as well, and how they met on their way here. It sounds most romantic! We'll have things to gossip about for months! Oh, there's someone at the door already. Go and answer it will you, Ginny? I expect it's the Hobsons. They're always first to arrive at everything in case they miss out. Now where did I put the salt?"

"It's there on the counter," Ginny pointed as she hurried out of the dining room.

★ ★ ★

Jarrod had changed into a clean shirt and clean pair of socks but had nothing else to wear to the party except his one pair of trousers and thin jacket. Would they be suitable or would people laugh at him behind his back? He was relieved when he saw that Brian Tyler was still wearing his same suit.

"Come on, Jarrod," Tyler said and together they went out into the darkening night. "Don't look so worried. It's me they want to see, me they want to talk to, my history they'll be interested in. You'll have a good time you see. If

I know anything there'll be plenty to eat and drink. Maybe someone will be playing a piano and you can perhaps find a nice young lady to waltz round the floor."

It didn't take them long to reach the Cox's house where lights showed in all the windows. Tyler led the way up to the door and knocked. A few moments later it was opened by Marshal Cox.

He ushered them in, took their coats, then opened the door on to a room where it seemed to Jarrod an awful lot of people had gathered. He clapped his hands.

"Everyone! I'd like to present our new preacher, Mr Brian Tyler."

Faces turned towards them, people began to gather round, wanting to shake hands, to ask the man about himself.

"And this is his friend, the man responsible for him getting here in one piece, Jarrod Kilkline."

"Jarrod?"

Above the sounds of the other people,

all greeting their new preacher, Jarrod clearly heard her voice. He didn't — couldn't — believe it. How could Ginny possibly be out here in Rock Springs? It wasn't possible. His heart began to hammer. He had to be wrong. Then he saw her pushing her way through the crowd.

"Jarrod!" she cried.

"Ginny! Ginny!"

And suddenly they were running towards one another, hugging tightly, while they both began to cry.

* * *

"Oh, Ginny, I can't believe I've found you again." Jarrod and Ginny sat together on the porch swing, the party for Tyler completely forgotten. "I thought I'd never see you again. Now I've met up with you here in the Rockies of all places!" He clutched at her hands, smiling at her.

"After I married Parker we didn't hear anything of you for so long and no one could tell us anything. The South was in a turmoil. We thought you must be dead. Otherwise I would never have left the farm, not even for Parker. I would have stayed until you came home however difficult it was."

"I don't think your being there would have made any difference. Our's wasn't the only farm ruined by the war. And with the Yanks having got the South under their goddamned thumb, it would have taken years to recover. Perhaps it never would. You did right leaving when you did. As long as you're happy."

"Of course I am."

But Jarrod wasn't so sure. Ginny no longer looked like the carefree girl she'd once been. She seemed as much changed to him as he must appear changed to her. Perhaps the war was to blame, perhaps it was Parker.

He wasn't surprised to find out that Ginny had married Parker Howland. Parker had always considered himself and the Howland family better than the Kilklines, and he and Jarrod had never been good friends. That hadn't stopped Parker hanging round the farm in order to speak to Ginny; and at church socials he'd always danced with her more than any of the other girls, much to their jealousy, because his looks and charm made them all sigh.

It was just a pity Parker couldn't have been content to follow in his father's footsteps and farm his land. But he'd always been cursed with big dreams and high hopes.

"I know it doesn't appear that we're doing all that well but it's not Parker's fault," Ginny defended her husband against Jarrod's implied criticism. "He tries so hard but he doesn't have a lot of luck or success."

Jarrod thought that was typical of Parker. But who was he to criticize? At least Parker wasn't wanted by the law.

"I can't believe how things have turned out," Ginny said with a sad sigh.

"It sure takes some getting used to

being an outlaw with a price on my head." Jarrod tried not to sound as bitter as he felt.

"Surely people will see that you didn't mean to do what you did and that you're sorry."

"I don't think that's much of an excuse. I robbed stagecoaches, Ginny. A man was killed."

"You didn't kill him."

"I was there. It doesn't make much difference who pulled the trigger."

"It does to me. Won't you be safe here? We're miles away from Arizona. No one knows you."

"I'll see."

"Please stay, Jarrod. For a while anyway. For your sake as well as mine. You look so weary. You'll be safe here. Mr Cox is a good town marshal but he isn't all that concerned about what goes on elsewhere."

"What if a new marshal comes along, one out to make a reputation for himself?"

"You should face that when it

happens, not before."

Jarrod sighed. "Perhaps you're right."

"Mr Tyler seems nice too. Couldn't he help you?"

"Maybe."

Ginny went on anxiously. "You could start up a farm again. This is good farming country. There's water, the soil is rich. It's free land too."

For a moment, although he didn't believe it would ever happen, Jarrod allowed himself to be caught up in his sister's dream, as much for her sake as for his. "It would be nice to have my own farm. But, Ginny, I'd need so much. Implements, a plough. Seed. A tent to live in until I could build a house. I can't afford it. I'm an outlaw but not a very successful one. I haven't got the money to buy any of those things. I haven't got hardly any money at all."

"If you stay you could earn money by helping Mr Tyler build his church. You don't have to get all the money all at once. There's plenty of odd jobs around if you look for them. People always want things built or repaired. That's what I'm always telling Parker but he doesn't take any notice. Don't you be stubborn like him, Jarrod."

"I'll think about it. Anyway," he bent to kiss her cheek, "I shan't be going just yet. I shan't just ride away and leave you."

* * *

Later in his room, Jarrod lay in bed wondering exactly what the hell he was going to do.

His intention had been to see what Rock Springs was like and then decide if, and how long, he would stay. He'd thought that it probably wouldn't be long before the safety of Utah and the Mormons beckoned.

Ginny being here changed all that. He couldn't just up, walk away and leave her. She was family. A reminder of home. Now he'd found her he didn't intend to lose her again.

If he stayed he'd have to get a job. And he'd have to stay out of trouble with the law.

★ ★ ★

"What we gonna do now?" Elmer Jackson whined. "All our money's gone."

"And whose fault was that?" Otis said accusingly.

Elmer didn't say any more. He was too scared of his oldest brother to openly criticize him. So too was Otis, normally, but now he was too angry to keep quiet. All that way, the harsh and dangerous journey, and for what? A couple of hours' pleasure! The fact that he'd also had a thoroughly good time in the arms of a red haired whore didn't really make up for having to slink penniless back to California.

"Shut up," Wilbur snarled. "Let me think."

"I didn't even get my new boots."

The preacher! What was it that Tyler

had said? Wilbur hadn't often listened to him as he went on about his religion. The Jacksons weren't exactly interested in that sort of thing. What was it? Something about the citizens of Rock Springs collecting money for a church.

Wilbur wasn't very smart but even he could figure out that while they'd sent the preacher twenty dollars for his journey, they must have collected a helluva lot more than that. Twenty dollars wouldn't build a church.

He grinned. Rock Springs was clearly a prosperous town.

"What is it?" Elmer asked. He didn't like it when his brother smiled in that mysterious way. It usually meant Wilbur was going to suggest something Elmer wouldn't understand and Wilbur would become impatient with him.

"We're off to Rock Springs in the morning."

Both Otis and Elmer looked at their brother as if he was mad.

Otis said, "But that's miles out of our way. It'll take us a couple of days at least. What the hell do we want to go there for?"

"What will those good citizens have to spend all their church money on now?"

Elmer considered this very carefully. "I don't know," he admitted, looking and sounding very puzzled.

Wilbur reached over to punch his arm. "Think, Elmer. They ain't got nothing to spend it on, not now their preacher is dead."

"Then what are they going to do with it?"

Wilbur sighed at Otis's question. It was difficult enough to think for himself, without having to think for two others as well. "They're gonna give it to us. Or rather we're going to relieve them of their useless burden."

He smiled. It wasn't a very nice smile. And as they realized what he meant his brothers grinned as well.

10

"YEAH, guy like you describe was here a few days ago," the store owner said.

Thank Christ for that, Lester Peabody thought. He hadn't been at all sure that he was still on the right trail. Because Mr Kilkline had suddenly taken it into his head not to go to Utah after all but instead to head out into the Rockies.

Why? Peabody couldn't guess. He'd long since given up trying to fathom out what went on in the mind of a wanted man; he'd simply followed. The long cold journey hadn't been helped when his horse put a leg in a hole and came up lame. The animal was just about better now but it had slowed him down. Kilkline was a long way ahead of him again.

"But he wasn't alone," the store owner added, much to Peabody's surprise.

"He wasn't?"

"No. He was with an older guy."

"What did he look like?"

"Oh, he was quite tall, bit plump, brown hair and a moustache."

"Did they act friendly?"

"Yeah. They weren't here long. Had some trouble over in the saloon and skedaddled out of town."

Peabody wasn't surprised by that. Trouble seemed to follow Jarrod Kilkline around. He made arrangements to sleep in the store's back room and then went over to the saloon to see what he could find out there.

He wondered who the other man with Kilkline could be. Was it Harry Phillips? It didn't really sound like him and, if it was, where had the pair of them met up and why were they so friendly? As far as Peabody knew Kilkline and Phillips, once companions on the owlhoot trail, were now enemies. Had something happened to change that again? Or was the man someone Kilkline had somehow met in the

101

mountains? He gave up worrying. It didn't really matter, and he'd find out soon enough.

★ ★ ★

As the saloon door opened, Ronnie Bennett's cruel mouth twisted into an ugly grin. Things had been quiet since the fight with the preacher and his friend a few days ago. It was time there was some more excitement around the place. And it looked as if the tinhorn just coming in was the type to provide it. Bennett didn't stop to wonder who the man was or what he was doing here, he just saw the opportunity to amuse himself.

"Lookee here," he said to Myra.

The girl, who still had the remains of a black eye and split lip from the beating Bennett had given her for 'encouraging' the preacher, felt her heart sink. "Please, Ronnie, don't cause any trouble."

"Trouble, sweetheart? Of course I

ain't gonna cause any trouble." He watched as Peabody went up to the bar and bought a beer. He wasn't the only one in the saloon watching the stranger. Most of the men present had never seen anyone quite like him before. "I'm just gonna have me some fun. Now why don't you go, be nice to him? Earn your living for a goddamned change."

Peabody had no illusions about the saloon or its occupants. He would have to watch his step. He sipped at his beer and then turned as someone touched his arm. A young girl stood by his side. She looked a poor, downtrodden scrap of a thing and for once he felt a momentary touch of pity at someone else's plight.

"Are you lonely, mister? Would you like some company?"

Peabody wasn't exactly lonely but it had been a long time since he'd had a woman. But he didn't want a child. "No, it's all right."

"Please, mister, my boyfriend won't

like it if you refuse."

Peabody had seen the girl's companion. A big bully of a miner. "Was it your boyfriend gave you that black eye?"

She nodded.

"Well if I pay him whatever you would normally cost, will that satisfy him?"

"I don't know."

"Let's see shall we?"

Peabody handed her some coins. She went and gave them to the big miner, who grinned. Putting his arm round the girl he got up and came over to the bar. "Ronnie Bennett," he introduced himself.

"Lester Peabody."

"You've travelled a long way ain't you? Come a bit out of your way? Perhaps you've lost your wagon train?" Several of the nearby men laughed at this piece of wit.

"No, I'm not lost. Can I buy you both a drink?"

"Yeah, sure. Double whiskey for me and a beer for the little lady here."

They took the drinks back to the table in the corner which Ronnie always sat at when he was in the place.

"What are you doing here then? Don't get many travellers through, especially at this time of the year."

Peabody had the feeling his occupation wouldn't go down too well with the saloon's customers. He hoped that Bennett, who had already downed his double whiskey, would be too befuddled to notice that he didn't reply. "I understand you had a bit of excitement here the other night?"

Myra stiffened. So she was the cause of the trouble.

"That's right. With some goddamned preacher and his pal."

"Preacher?" This was getting stranger by the minute.

"Or at least that's what the bastard said he was. Ain't that right?" And Bennett pinched Myra's arm making her squeal in pain and making Peabody want to hit him.

"He was a preacher," Myra protested

faintly. "I've already told you that. We were talking, we weren't doing anything else."

Peabody decided Bennett was both dangerous, and unpredictable, if on one night he was willing to sell his girlfriend to a stranger and on another beat her up for selling herself.

"What happened when they left here?"

"Dunno," Bennett shrugged. "I didn't give chase. They weren't worth it."

Probably because poor Myra was the easier victim.

"They were on their way to Rock Springs, ain't that what the *preacher* said?"

Myra nodded reluctantly.

"Where's that?"

"On the other side of the mountains. Near Denver. Hey? Why are you asking all these questions?"

"Oh no real reason. Buy you another drink?"

★ ★ ★

106

Lester Peabody lay on the narrow, uncomfortable and probably bug infested bed in the back of the store, mulling things over. So Jarrod Kilkline had somehow, and for some reason, hooked up with a man who was meant to be a preacher. And they were headed for a town called Rock Springs.

So he would go there too. Even if Kilkline had already left, it should prove easy enough to pick up another clue as to where he had gone.

Peabody's thoughts were abruptly disturbed. A sound reached his sharp ears. That of a creaky floorboard from somewhere within the store. Not the store owner. He slept upstairs. Someone from the saloon?

The door crashed open. By the faint light coming from the small window in the back room, he saw Ronnie Bennett outlined against the open doorway. With a roar, Bennett leapt towards him, giving Peabody no time to do anything but roll over the side of the bed. He landed on the floor with a painful thump while Bennett landed on the empty bed. Bennett was the first to recover and as Peabody struggled to his feet, the man came rushing up to him, grabbing his hair and jerking him to his feet.

"Eastern greenhorn!" he yelled as if that was some sort of crime.

Peabody was punched and thrown to the floor. He knew he could never beat the big miner in a fight, fair or otherwise. Heart pounding, he forced himself to act calmly. He had, after all, been in this sort of situation before.

He picked himself up and as Bennett stepped into the attack again, he reached down, towards his calf. His hand enclosed on the small but comforting derringer he kept strapped to his leg. Bennett grabbed him again but Peabody already had the gun out. He raised it, pressed it against Bennett's forehead and pulled the trigger.

Bennett screamed as the gun exploded in his face. He staggered back. The hole left in his forehead might only have been tiny but fired that close it was also fatal. The miner clutched at his eyes, fell heavily, twitched once or twice and then was still.

Breathing hard Peabody stood holding the gun at his side. At the same time, the store owner, followed by several others from the nearby buildings, crowded into the room.

"What the hell is going on?" That was the bartender, Rogers, from the saloon.

"Bennett was trying to kill me," Peabody tried to explain.

"You shot him!" the store owner accused.

"He left me no choice. He attacked me."

"Lock him up!"

"Hey now, wait a goddamned minute," Peabody protested angrily. "It was self defence."

"That's as maybe," Rogers said. "Bennett's friends are out of town right now but they come back and find Ronnie dead and we did nothing about his killer we'll be the ones in trouble."

"They'll kill me for what wasn't my fault."

"We don't hold you, mister, they'll kill us."

Peabody realized the futility of arguing. The derringer was taken from him and he was manhandled out of the store, across the yard and into the saloon. Several of the men took the opportunity to kick or hit him; probably not because they were upset at Bennett's death but because they wanted to hurt someone who was different to them. He didn't struggle or protest.

The saloon girls, Myra amongst them, were standing on the stairs, waiting to see what the commotion was all about.

"Bennett's dead," the bartender called up to Myra.

One of the other whores put an arm round the girl but if anyone expected her to be shocked or upset by the man's sudden death, they were mistaken. Myra felt only relief.

A door at the end of the bar was opened. Beyond was darkness. Peabody was shoved forward. He found himself falling down a short but steep flight of steps into the cellar below. He scraped his elbows and knees. And even as he came to a halt at the bottom, the door was slammed shut, leaving him in complete blackness.

11

BREAKFAST was served by Mrs Goodman at eight o'clock sharp, the guests sitting at one long table in the dining room. The breakfast plates were piled high with bacon, eggs, beans and thick slices of home-baked bread, and there was as much coffee as anyone wanted.

Jarrod hoped no one noticed how much he ate. Life in both the Confederate Army and since, had taught him to eat as much as he could whenever he could, because the next meal wasn't always certain.

"What are you going to do today, Mr Tyler?" Ginny asked.

"I believe the Marshal and Mr Hobson have some plans of the church to show me. Then they're going to take me around and show me the sites they think would be most suitable for it."

"But the final decision will be yours?"

"Yes."

"I'm sure you'll make the right one."

"I hope so, Mrs Howland."

"At least you've arrived in the Spring. It's a lovely day."

Tyler looked out of the window. The sun was shining and the wind had dropped. Perhaps Rock Springs wasn't so bad a place after all. He hoped that his more cheerful disposition didn't have anything to do with meeting Ginny Howland; she was a happily married woman after all, but he rather feared it did. Any feelings he might have for her would have to be squashed and quickly.

He didn't mind breaking some of the Ten Commandments but, so far, he hadn't felt the need to covet his neighbour's wife. He didn't intend to do so now.

"What about you, Jarrod?"

"I'll stay with Ginny. We've still got so much to talk about."

"Good idea. Where's Parker this morning?"

Ginny didn't like to say that her husband had drunk rather too much of Mrs Cox's punch and was sleeping it off. Yet she didn't like to lie either. "He'll be up and about soon," she said and was relieved when Tyler didn't ask her any more.

"Perhaps I can meet up with you all later. I'll treat you to lunch."

★ ★ ★

"I'll have to go soon," Marshal Cox said, nevertheless pausing to pour himself out another cup of coffee. "I'm meeting the preacher and Mr Hobson."

"What do you think of Mr Tyler?" Naomi asked.

Cox grinned. "He's not exactly what anyone expected, is he? Did you see Mr Hobson's face when Tyler was telling everyone about the robbery and he let out a few goddamns and sonsofbitches?"

"I thought Mrs Hobson was going to faint! But someone like Mr Tyler is just the sort of preacher a place like Rock Springs needs."

"It's not Tyler I'm worried about." Cox frowned. "It's his companion."

"Oh?"

Cox had spent time the day before looking through his collection of Wanted posters. Not all that many reached his remote spot and he hadn't found one for Jarrod Kilkline. That didn't mean one didn't exist.

"Well, I thought it was lovely that Ginny has found her brother again. She's often spoken about him to me and she believed he was dead. It would be a shame if you had to do anything to spoil her new found happiness."

Cox sighed, sensing domestic discomfort. "Well so far he's done nothing that I know of. But if I learn that he's broken the law then I'll have no choice but to arrest him."

Naomi snorted, showing her husband

exactly what she sometimes thought of the law.

★ ★ ★

"These are the plans Mr Hobson has drawn up for the church." Marshal Cox spread several pieces of paper out on the desk so that Tyler could study them.

"I hope you find them satisfactory," Mr Hobson preened. It had been his idea for the town to hire its own preacher and in the middle of his office, in pride of place, were the church plans he'd drawn up. Not that he was an architect but as the Mayor he'd designated himself the most suitable person for the task. He'd also decided to pick out personally Mr Tyler's application from the few they'd received. He wasn't quite sure how he viewed his choice. Brian Tyler was nothing like the preachers he remembered from his youth in the East.

Tyler rather liked some of the more fanciful designs. But, knowing that funds were limited, decided upon one that was plain and simple, and which would be more in keeping with the surroundings. Perhaps, later on, there would be the opportunity to add pinnacles, a church tower, bells and fancy embellishments.

"We thought you'd want the church to be as close to the town as possible," Cox said. "But at the same time have room for a house, a new cemetery and somewhere where socials can be held."

"My idea exactly," Tyler replied, pleased that so much thought had gone into what he might want. He was also pleased to learn that the town planned to build him his own house. Living at the boarding house was all right, but he preferred some privacy.

Followed by most of the town's dignitaries, as well as the idle curious, he spent the morning surveying the places picked out as possible sites for his church, while the Marshal and Mr Hobson pointed out the merits of each.

In the end, he decided on the rise to the east of the town near the creek that ran through the hills, and which eventually became the springs that gave the town its name.

"That way the church will be seen from miles away by those coming into town."

It also offered one of the best views across the creek and was farthest away from the encroaching mountains, which Tyler feared he would never become used to.

"At least we won't have far to go to get the lumber," Cox said with a smile and a wave of his hand at the pine trees. "And we've got several people in town experienced in cutting timber. I reckon, now that the weather has improved, we can get started right away."

"Good. And in the meantime I'll hold Sunday services either in the courthouse or in the yard at the back."

It was washday at the boarding house and, in order to earn some money, Ginny usually helped the overworked Mrs Goodman.

"Does she want me to do anything?" Jarrod asked.

Ginny laughed. "No. Washday is woman's work. You'd only be in the way. Why don't you keep Parker company? Make sure he stays out of trouble."

"You haven't told him anything about me, have you?"

Ginny squeezed her brother's arm. "No, that's our secret."

Recovered from the effects of the punch, Parker had rather hoped to go to the saloon, but was reluctantly willing instead to accompany his brother-in-law round the town, showing him its very few sights.

"I don't know what Ginny really thinks of it here," Parker admitted as they came to a halt in some rocks above the swift running creek.

"Unfortunately we arrived at the start of winter so it hasn't exactly been easy but the last few days she's seemed much happier. And of course seeing you again has bucked her up no end. She's starting to drop hints about having her own house again and starting a family."

"Is that so surprising?" Jarrod asked.

"Not really. I suppose it's what I want too. The trouble is I'd need a proper job for that. But I like gambling and I'm good at it. I don't know that I want to do anything else."

"You're going to help Mr Tyler build his church though, aren't you?"

Parker grimaced. "Ginny tells me I've got to. Perhaps if I work hard on that I'll earn enough money so we can at least hire a couple of rooms for the time being. And wait for things to go back to normal. But that's another problem."

"What is?"

"Well, Mr Tyler seems reasonable

enough but once he's installed in his own church he might decide he doesn't approve of gambling or drinking. He might demand the closure of the saloons."

"Oh, I don't think there's any fear of that," Jarrod said with a grin, remembering his companion's strange habits. "Parker," he turned away from the rocks, "Ginny wants me to stay here. Think about taking up farming again. You were once a farmer too. Would you consider coming in with me?" He realized he was holding his breath waiting for Parker's answer.

"I don't know. I hoped to leave farming behind me. Maybe, if I have luck gambling I could put money into the place. But, Jarrod, I know I've hurt Ginny many times in the past. I expect I'll hurt her again in the future. But I don't want you hurting her as well by promising her something you won't be able to honour."

"What do you mean?" Jarrod asked angrily.

"Are you sure you'll be able to stay here?"

Jarrod sighed. Was it that obvious that he was on the run from the law?

"Are you in any position to promise her anything at the moment?"

"No."

12

SUN with real warmth in it shone down on the workers in the meadow. The sky above was a clear blue. Spring had arrived.

The church was already quickly taking shape. While some of the men skilled in logging went into the pine forests to cut the best timber they could find, others loaded it into wagons and carted it back to the site. There the air was full of the sound of men cutting and sawing the timber into the required lengths and the smell of the freshly cut wood.

The work was overseen by Mr Hobson who fussed around to make sure his designs were followed carefully.

When the building was finished it would be painted white. Inside an altar would be placed beneath the western facing window, there would be a choir stall should there ever be enough singers to make a choir, and several pews. Tyler intended to go to Denver as soon as he could to buy Bibles and a pair of candles to place either side of the altar's silver cross. There wasn't enough for any other fancy trimmings.

It would, Tyler knew, be a little crude at first but a lot of hard work was going into its building; it was a labour of love.

Tyler was worried that if he got too complacent and pleased with himself something would go wrong to bring him back down to earth, but it was difficult not to believe that God was happy with his choice of location for the church.

★ ★ ★

"Rock Springs should be over the next rise," Wilbur Jackson said. "You remember what we decided don't you?"

"Yeah, we ride in and out as quick as

we can, without attracting attention," said Otis. "It ain't necessary for you to keep telling me and Elmer what to do. We ain't stupid."

Wilbur sighed and wondered, not for the first time, whether to ride off and leave his brothers to fend for themselves. He just hoped he wasn't expecting them to bite off more than they could chew. The beating and robbing of the preacher wasn't the first of their crimes. Stealing from lone travellers or isolated country stores was their style. None of them had much idea of how to go about robbing a town.

"Where d'you think the money will be?"

"Dunno, exactly, Elmer. If there ain't a bank it'll still be kept somewhere official. Mebbe the lawman's office." None of them felt very hopeful about that; the Jacksons and the law didn't go very well together. "We should be able to find some friendly person willing to tell us, especially when we put a gun to his ear."

Elmer laughed. "We 'bout ready to go?"

"Yeah. And," Wilbur felt a further word of warning was necessary even if his brothers didn't take much notice of it, "no gunplay if it can be helped. Now let's move!"

★ ★ ★

Ginny and Parker were arguing again. It seemed to Ginny that it was all they'd done during the last couple of days and she just hoped that Mrs Goodman couldn't hear.

"Aren't you going to help Mr Tyler with the church today?" she asked, watching as Parker tied his new scarlet bandanna round his neck, patting its folds carefully into shape.

"No."

"Why?"

"Because I'm fed up is why. I've worked hard for him and his damn church . . ."

"Parker," Ginny protested.

126

" . . . And I haven't had any thanks from him or from you."

"That's not true. I don't know what you're talking about."

It was on the tip of Parker's tongue to say something about the way in which Tyler gazed at Ginny when he thought no one was looking, or about how she smiled at him. But to do so would be to admit to something he didn't want to acknowledge and would plunge them into more misery. Instead, acknowledging his other grievance, he said sulkily, "What's Jarrod doing? You must know, you've been spending so much time with him lately."

So that was it, Ginny thought, or at least it was part of their trouble. "You can't possibly be jealous of Jarrod. We haven't seen each other for such a long time and he's my brother."

"And he's never thought me good enough for you."

"Now you're being silly."

"I'd better go." And Parker walked away before he could say anything more. He knew he was being childish but he couldn't help himself.

Ginny sighed, watching him go. She wiped a tear from her eyes. Naomi Cox would be here any minute and she didn't want the woman to know she was upset.

★ ★ ★

"Have you thought any more about what you're going to do?" Tyler asked as he passed Jarrod some nails, and watched the young man begin to hammer them home. They were up a ladder working on the church roof.

"Not really. We've been so busy here I haven't had a chance."

"It won't be long before the church is finished," Tyler warned.

"I know. Mrs Goodman has asked if I'll build her a shed in her yard afterwards. She said I could stay on free of charge while I did so. It'll take me about a month. I think I will."

"Good. And have you thought any

more about starting up a farm? Ginny, er, your sister, er, Mrs Howland, would like you to. She's spoken to me about it more than once."

"Trying to get you to influence me, huh?"

"It sounds good to me."

"I haven't got the money right now and Parker seems to have gone off the idea of lending me any. But if I could I wouldn't mind giving it a try. Although a farm here in the Rockies wouldn't be quite the same as the family farm back home in Georgia."

"It would at least be a farm. Sometimes, Jarrod, we have to make the most of what we've got."

"I know."

"I can't say that Rock Springs came quite up to my expectations. But the people are good and kind and I intend to do what I can for them."

"Things don't always work out how we want."

"The best is all we can do. Ah, it looks like company."

"Hello!"

Jarrod looked down from his labours to see Ginny and Naomi Cox toiling up the slope towards them. They were carrying baskets full of lemonade and pies.

"Food! Good! Let's go and eat, Jarrod, we deserve a break."

Jarrod followed the preacher. He didn't miss the way the man's face lit up when he saw Ginny. Neither did he miss how Tyler fussed round her at the boarding house, nor the way Ginny didn't seem to mind. He had the feeling that Parker had noticed it too and that was why he was acting so moodily. Jarrod wondered if he should say anything. But what could he say? What harm was there in a few quick glances? Ginny would never act improperly; nor would Brian Tyler. Parker would have to solve his own problems, many of which were of his own making.

"How long do you think it'll be before the church is ready?" Ginny asked, when she and Mrs Cox had handed round the food. She gazed up at the building. "It looks fine."

"Everyone is working so hard it'll soon be complete," Tyler replied. "Wait," he added, putting out a hand to stop her, although he knew he shouldn't, "don't go for a moment. Sit down." He moved to make room for her on the log on which he had perched.

"All right." Ginny smiled at him.

Jarrod wasn't the only one to notice things. Unseen by anyone, Parker had followed his wife up to the meadow. He told himself he wasn't spying on her, that he meant to help with the work, join in with the picnic. But now he watched jealously as Ginny poured Tyler out some lemonade. He stepped back into the shadows of a pine tree.

He no longer wanted anything to eat or drink. In fact what he wanted to do was hit the preacher in the face; that would stop him laughing with Ginny.

Well they could all go hang — the

preacher, Jarrod, Ginny, Rock Springs — he would no longer help with the church. He'd do exactly what he wanted. And right now he wanted to go to the saloon and see if he could find anyone to play cards with.

13

IT was quiet when the Jackson brothers rode into Rock Springs. The activities of the day had finished and those of the night not yet started. A few people were still around but no one they need worry about. Wilbur came to a halt in the middle of Main Street, Otis and Elmer following suit. He looked round. Unfortunately, the town didn't seem to have a bank and he didn't want to go to the Marshal's office if he could help it.

"Wilbur," Otis began. He could see what looked like the spire of a church in the distance. Surely if Wilbur was right, he had to be mistaken. Why would the people of Rock Springs be building a church if they didn't have a preacher? But if, for some strange reason, they were building one, then what had happened to the money? He had a sudden horrible feeling about this.

Wilbur took no notice. His eyes had lit on the real estate office. It was the only place of business still open. It also looked the newest and most substantial building along the street and it seemed to Wilbur that whoever owned it considered himself as important as his office and would surely know where the money was.

★ ★ ★

Mr Hobson was about to call it a day. He could have called it a day almost as soon as he opened up that morning. He was hopeful that sometime soon there would be an influx of families wanting to buy some real estate but business wasn't exactly brisk. Mrs Hobson was starting to get fed up waiting, especially when a lot of their own money had gone into promoting the town.

When the door opened, he looked up with a businesslike smile on his face, a smile that faltered and died as he saw the three men who sauntered in. They didn't look like customers, or not the sort he wanted to deal with anyway.

Nevertheless, in case appearances were deceptive, he said, "C . . . can I help you?"

"Where is it?" Wilbur asked.

"Where's what?" Mr Hobson was bewildered.

"The money."

Oh damn, it was a robbery!

"I haven't got any money. No one's buying land these days and . . . "

"Shut it!" Otis said menacingly.

"Not your money you old fool," Wilbur added. "The money to build the church."

"Yeah I wanna buy me some new boots. Come on, quick, old man."

Mr Hobson didn't understand any of this. How did these men know about the church money? Who were they? Then, with sinking heart, he remembered the preacher's story about the three men who'd tricked him. Oh, please, he thought, don't let these be them but he knew they were.

What were they going to do? Especially when they found out there was hardly anything worth stealing. There hadn't been much money to start with, the citizens were relying on the land roundabout for most of their raw material, and some of it had gone to Mr Tyler for his journey. Even now Mrs Cox and his own wife were thinking of ways of raising more so the wages of the men working on the building could be paid. Mr Hobson had a feeling these three men wouldn't believe that.

"But I don't have it," he said in a voice quavering with fear.

"Then," Wilbur said, "you'd better tell us where it is, and fast." And he nodded at Otis, who was ever eager to get violent.

Stepping forward, Otis hit Mr Hobson round the face, hard, splitting the man's lip and sending him sprawling back against the wall. Mr Hobson cried out in pain and fright, grabbing at his desk to stop himself from falling. As Otis raised his fist to hit him again, the man flinched away and pleaded.

"Don't, please. Don't. It's not here. Please believe me. I haven't got it."

"Then where the hell is it?" Wilbur demanded.

"The Marshal has it, locked up, safe. You won't be able to get at it."

"Damn! Make sure he's telling the truth."

And Otis hit Mr Hobson again; this time the man collapsed to the floor, moaning.

★ ★ ★

Parker Howland had spent most of the afternoon drinking alone, there being no one in the saloon to play cards with. Now he wasn't exactly drunk but he was working himself up into a bad mood, thinking morosely about his ill fortune of the last few months, blaming everyone but himself for it.

Suddenly he slammed his glass down,

much to the surprise of the saloon's few other occupants. Dammit, this was stupid! Ginny was his wife! He'd go back to the boarding house right now and have it out with her. Demand to know what she felt for that damn preacher. Get her to choose between him or Tyler, and she'd damn well better choose him!

A little unsteady on his feet, he left the saloon. As he walked by the real estate office, he came to a halt, a little surprised to see it was still open. Wondering if Mr Hobson was all right, he opened the door and looked in.

He said, "Hello there," just as Otis and Elmer both kicked the man, who was lying helplessly on the floor. "Oh my God!" Parker was aware of a third man standing just behind the door. Scared into sudden sobriety, he dashed back out into the street, yelling, "Thieves! They're robbing Mr Hobson!"

"Shit!" Wilbur swore and without really thinking he drew his gun and fired. Wilbur wasn't particularly good with a gun but at that range he couldn't miss.

The bullet struck Parker in the centre of his back. He gave a little moan of pain, his legs seemed to get tangled up with one another and he fell face downward in the street. He tried to get up and couldn't. "Ginny," he whispered or at least he thought he spoke his wife's name.

"Jesus Christ!" Otis said. "Wilbur! What the hell have you done?"

For a moment Wilbur looked at the unmoving body in the road. "It weren't my fault," he whined. "He surprised me." From somewhere he heard a shout and a door banging open. "Let's get the hell outta here! Quick!"

The three men dashed for their horses.

★ ★ ★

Although the streets of Rock Springs had once echoed to shots and gunfights, both night and day, nowadays there was seldom any real trouble. Thus it took Gus Wilkinson a moment or two to realize that the shot from somewhere outside was a shot fired in anger. He got to his feet so fast the chair fell over and, cursing, he fumbled for his gun, somehow making it to the door without tripping over anything.

Where was Marshal Cox? At 5 o'clock sharp the man had stood up and said, "Think I'll go and make sure everything is locked up tight." He did and said the same every day. You could set your clock by him. Was the shot anything to do with him? Had he been hurt?

Heart beating frantically, Gus went out onto the street, having to step quickly back as three men, bent low over their horses' backs, urging their animals on, galloped by. He was so surprised and frightened he didn't even have time to get off one shot before they'd gone. Beyond, along Main Street, people were standing, staring, running out of the buildings to see what was going on.

Someone called, "Robbers! They were robbing Mr Hobson!"

Gus ran down the street towards the real estate office. And came to a halt. Marshal Cox, gun out, was approaching from the other end of town.

Then Gus saw Parker Howland lying on the ground, arms outstretched, several men bent over him. One of them looked up to shake his head and even Gus, inexperienced as he was, could see that Parker was dead.

14

"OH God, Jarrod, look!" Tyler pointed down to where a crowd had gathered. Marshal Cox was trying to restore order, calling for volunteers for a posse at the same time. "It looks like Parker!"

"Oh no." Jarrod broke into as fast a run as his limp would allow.

As he got closer he could see Ginny being supported by Naomi Cox and Mrs Goodman, while Mr Hobson, his face bloody from a cut over his eye, lingered nearby. Someone had laid a coat over Parker. From the way Ginny was weeping and the actions of the crowd he had no doubt that Parker was dead. "Ginny!" he called.

She pulled away from the women and flung herself into her brother's arms. "Oh, Jarrod, they shot Parker!"

she sobbed. "He's dead. What am I going to do?"

"What happened?" Tyler demanded.

"There were three men," Gus explained. "They tried to rob Mr Hobson."

"They mentioned the church money," Mr Hobson added.

"Dammit," Tyler breathed, knowing exactly who the three men were.

Jarrod glanced over Ginny's head to where Cox was getting his posse together. Several men had volunteered. Not only was everyone in an uproar over the shooting but it had been a long, boring winter. Here was the chance of some excitement. Should he stay with Ginny or go after Parker's killers?

"Gus!" Cox called. "We'll need water, provisions and blankets. See there's enough for everyone. Come with me, all of you, and I'll swear you in as deputies."

Jarrod's mind was made up. "Ginny, sweetheart, I'll have to go with them."

"Jarrod, don't!" Ginny clung to him. "Don't leave me."

"I must."

"It's all right," Naomi Cox said. "Ginny will be safe with us. Ginny, dear, you must let Jarrod go." Gently she took the girl in her arms.

Tyler wished he could go with the posse as well. He owed them damn Jacksons for himself — now he owed them for someone else's life as well. But he knew where his duty lay. He said to Jarrod, "I'll look after her. You know that if there's anything I can do for Ginny, or for you, you only have to ask."

"Yeah, I do." Jarrod kissed Ginny's cheek then without pausing to look back, hurried down to the livery stable where the owner was helping saddle the horses. His head was in a spin. He couldn't believe what had happened. Everything had been going so well, and now here in the space of moments Parker was dead and Ginny left a widow. Life sure wasn't fair.

He led his horse out into the road and swung up in the saddle. Digging heels into the animal's side he rode to where Marshal Cox was getting ready to lead the men out after the Jacksons.

* * *

The Jacksons rode on through the ever gathering gloom, fear driving them on. Once, when they came to the end of a long upsweeping valley they paused to look back. Far behind them a spiral of dust lingered on the air. They didn't doubt it was made by a posse.

But Wilbur knew that however long they could go on, the horses had to rest. It would be disastrous to be left afoot. So once they got amongst the trees again, he came to a halt. Taking hold of his canteen, he gulped down some water. He still couldn't believe he'd done such a foolish thing. Killed a man! Just like that. He was always accusing his brothers of behaving stupidly and here he was having shot someone in the back.

"Hell!" he said angrily. "Don't look at me like that! It was an accident. I never meant to do it. The silly bastard took me by surprise!"

"And now we've got a posse on our trail," said Otis, stating the obvious.

"What we gonna do?" Elmer moaned. He looked all round as if he expected their pursuers to suddenly spring out of the trees. "I'm real scared, Wilbur. You won't let us be killed, will you?"

"They ain't caught up with us yet. We move fast we can outrun 'em." Wilbur spoke more confidently than he truly felt. They didn't know these mountains. It was likely there were men with the posse who knew them well. "Besides," he added, "if they don't have luck soon, I bet they'll give up and go home."

Otis made a rude noise. "I doubt that. It ain't like we just robbed the store, or beat someone up. You murdered that man. They ain't about to forget that."

"All right, all right." Wilbur was getting angry again.

"Rock Springs used to be a tough mining town," Otis added. "If any of those miners are still around, it won't take much for the posse to turn into a lynch mob."

"Oh God," Elmer moaned.

"I said it was an accident. It's done now and over."

"It ain't over." Otis wasn't prepared to forget and forgive. "It ain't fair. It ain't like Elmer and me were the ones pulled the trigger. That was you, Wilbur."

Wilbur caught hold of his brother's coat collar and stuck his face close to Otis's. "You know damn well that won't matter to the good folks of Rock Springs. You'll be blamed just as much as me."

That was what Otis meant, it wasn't fair! They hadn't even got any money. But Otis didn't dare point that out.

Wilbur was in a bad enough mood as it was.

* * *

"How is she?" Mrs Goodman asked as Brian Tyler came out of Ginny's room.

He had stayed with her, sitting by the bed, holding her hand, just as Jarrod used to do during their childhood when Ginny was scared or upset. "She's asleep now."

"That'll be best. Poor little thing."

"I wish I could take her pain as my own."

Mrs Goodman had seen the way things were shaping up between the preacher and Mrs Howland. Being a good Christian lady she hadn't approved. But now things were different and her kind heart made her feel sorry for them both. "No one can do that, Mr Tyler. All you can do is wait with her and give her your support. She needs you."

"Right now that gives me no comfort. I'm so sorry for what happened. I feel responsible."

"It's not your fault. You couldn't have known those Jacksons would come here."

But Tyler shook his head. He should have obeyed his own first instincts about the three brothers — and not trusted them. Instead he'd been so eager to get to Rock Springs he'd pushed his feelings aside, and been so eager about his new church, he'd spoken out of turn. Now this was the result. It would be a long time before he forgave himself.

15

LESTER PEABODY knew he was in deeper trouble than he'd ever been before, and he'd been in some tight spots since he'd started chasing outlaws.

He wasn't even sure how long he'd been locked in the cellar. Time — whether it was day or night — had no meaning for him for it was too dark to see anything. But he was quite sure it wouldn't be long now before Ronnie Bennett's friends returned to the hamlet and that when they did they would kill him.

And, unless some sort of miracle happened, he couldn't see what he could do to prevent it.

Unable to see anything, he hadn't dared move too far away from the bottom of the stairs where he'd landed for fear he wouldn't make it back to them; and they, and the door at the top, were surely the only way out of the cellar.

Once or twice someone remembered he was down here and the door opened and food and drink, dry bread and water only, but welcome all the same, were put on the top step. He rather thought it was the girl, Myra, who was responsible but it all happened so quickly he wasn't sure and there hadn't been time to call out.

Several times he tried climbing the stairs and pushing at the door but it was always locked as he'd feared it would be. Although he banged on it and cried out for help, he didn't even know if anyone could hear him. No one took any notice.

What a place to go out in, he thought, feeling both anger and dismay, but not fright. He'd known from the start that his job was dangerous, the danger had been part of the attraction, and that it was quite likely to get him killed sooner or later. Better that than ending up being badly injured or dying of old age.

But he'd rather hoped that he would die in a blazing gunfight, taking several bad guys with him, and that his heroism would be reported in all the newspapers. He wanted his name to go down in the history books. He didn't want to be murdered in some no-account no-name town, where no one would ever learn what had happened to him.

"Mr Peabody. Mr Peabody."

He must have fallen asleep. He was lying on his side, head rested on his arms. The voice intruded into his dreams.

"Mr Peabody."

He opened his eyes, lifting his head. The door at the top of the stairs was open. He could see the flickering of a candle — so it had to be night — but not the person who held it. Were Bennett's friends here? No. It couldn't be them. They would come crashing down into the cellar to kick and punch him before taking him out to kill him.

"Who is it?"

"Me, Myra. Hurry please."

Peabody didn't hesitate. This might be some sort of trick. Equally it might not. He'd take the chance, because he had nothing to lose. He scrambled up the stairs. The girl was dressed in a skirt and jacket, quite unlike her working clothes, and she was alone, the rest of the room in darkness. The hand holding the candle shook so much he quickly took it from her, for fear that she would drop it and start a fire; although perhaps burning the saloon and the whole damn town wasn't such a bad idea.

"I came to help you as soon as I could. Up until tonight Mr Rogers has slept down here to keep an eye out and I couldn't do anything."

Peabody still suspected a trick. "Why isn't he here tonight?"

Myra shrugged. "I'm not sure. We did hear that Ronnie's friends are on

153

their way back and most everybody got drunk. I think Mr Rogers did too and he's sleeping it off. Does it matter?" she added impatiently. "He ain't here and so I can help you."

"Why do you want to help me? I shot your boyfriend."

"He thought he was my boyfriend, I didn't. Now are you going to escape or are you going to spend all night jawing?" There was impatience in her voice again.

Peabody grinned. "I'm going to escape."

"Good. I managed to get your things from the store when you were first brought here and no one was taking any notice of me and what I did. I hope I got everything."

"It doesn't matter. You got enough." Peabody flung on his coat and boots, securing about himself his various weapons. "Is my horse at the livery?"

Myra nodded. "I thought it was safest to leave it there." She put out a hand to stop the man as he went to go outside. "Mr Peabody, I sure hope you ain't thinking of leaving me behind."

Peabody stopped. That was exactly what he had intended. He hadn't thought about the girl beyond the fact that she had rescued him and so allowed him both to escape and to get on with chasing Jarrod Kilkline.

"Ronnie's friends will figure out it's me who let you go. They won't take kindly to that. You can't leave me behind."

Peabody hesitated. Myra meant nothing to him. She was a whore. Kilkline was all that mattered. Yet she had helped him. At undoubted risk to herself. For once he let his heart rule his head.

"All right," he said. "Come on."

The girl's body sagged in relief. As she followed him to the door, she said. "Where are we going?"

"Rock Springs."

16

IT was the morning of the third day. The posse was still on the trail of the Jackson brothers and getting closer all the time.

It hadn't been an easy ride. The rocky hillsides were choked with brush and tall grass, the pine trees pressing so close in places it was almost impossible to find a way through. And Cox had kept them moving, allowing them only short breaks during the day, keeping going at night until it was dark, getting them up early in the morning.

Evidently the Jacksons didn't know where they were going. They'd had to backtrack several times. Thanks to Gus Wilkinson, who was a skilled tracker, the three men were now only a couple of hours ahead and there was a panicky feel to their actions.

Around mid-morning Marshal Cox called a short halt. He dismounted with a groan, thinking he was getting too old for this sort of thing. Everything ached. "I reckon we'll have 'em in our sights before long."

"I hope so." Jarrod was scared that if they didn't catch up soon, the others would start getting edgy and want to return to Rock Springs, although, so far, there was no sign of that.

While there were a few grumbles at the pace Cox set, the men were still as eager as Jarrod to catch up with Parker's murderers.

He kept wondering what was happening back in town and how Ginny was bearing up and if he should have stayed with her. At least she wasn't alone. She had the support of Naomi Cox and Mrs Goodman; and the Reverend Tyler.

"Don't worry, Jarrod, we'll arrest 'em and soon." And when they did Cox intended to keep an eye on the young man. Although Jarrod had behaved himself in Rock Springs, causing no trouble, working hard, the Marshal still wasn't certain about him. Jarrod had a quick temper, perhaps it was that what had gotten him into trouble before, and Cox didn't want him, or any of them, throwing hanging ropes over tree branches.

Under the warm sun, the posse rode on for another couple of hours. Gus was riding along in front studying the ground. Gradually the undergrowth thinned out, enabling them to see farther ahead.

"Look!" Jarrod suddenly cried, pointing.

The three Jacksons had appeared on the ridge of the hill in front of them. They were skylined.

"Go to it, Gus," Cox ordered. "Quick."

"What about me?" Jarrod demanded.

"Gus is a good shot. Accurate with a rifle."

"So am I."

"He spends time each day in

target practice."

"Shooting a man is altogether different to shooting at a tin can. I hope he don't muff his chance."

While this argument had been going on, Gus got off his horse and pulling his rifle from its scabbard, laid it across the saddlehorn.

Cox added a piece of advice. "Just remember what they done. And that it's your job to stop 'em any way you can. Do your best, son."

"OK, Marshal." Gus too hoped he wouldn't fail. A lot of the townspeople considered him young and arrogant, he didn't want to give them an excuse to sack him. This was his chance to prove they were wrong.

But it was a long shot to make.

He leaned against his horse, lining up the rifle on the ridge. He aimed at the third man, the nearest and the slowest moving. As everyone else held their breath, he squeezed the trigger and fired.

For a moment he thought he'd

missed. Then the man flung up his arms and fell off his horse.

★ ★ ★

Parker's funeral was to be held later that morning.

"At least you're here, Mr Tyler," Mrs Goodman said. "You can give poor Parker a decent burial. That'll be a comfort to Ginny. I wish the Marshal would get back with all three of them murderers. I shan't feel happy until they've been tried and sentenced. And I hope they're hung!" Obviously fearing that Tyler would find her opinion unladylike, the woman blushed and hid her confusion by passing him the coffeepot.

Tyler was relieved when Ginny put in an appearance. But Ginny was used to hardship, there had been plenty of that back on the Georgia farm. She knew that, however sad she felt, she had to get on with her life. No one would be pleased if she decided to remain in bed, just because Parker was being buried and she couldn't go on without him.

As she sat down Tyler thought how wan she looked. Naomi Cox had lent her a black dress and it was too big for her, making it look as if she had lost a lot of weight. He put a hand over her's and she didn't try to remove it.

"It'll be all right," he said. "I'll be there."

* * *

"Elmer! Elmer!" Otis yelled as his brother landed on the ground. "Wilbur, Elmer's been shot!"

Wilbur muttered something that sounded like 'Shit' and getting off his horse followed Otis to where Elmer lay on his back. The young man was clutching at his shoulder, blood spurting through his fingers and down his arm. His eyes were open and he looked pitifully at Wilbur and Otis.

"It hurts. I'm shot. Help me. I'm dying."

"No, you ain't," Wilbur said unsympathetically.

Elmer moaned. How could Wilbur say that? He wasn't the one shot. It hurt, like hell, and it surely felt like he was dying.

Wilbur glanced down their backtrail and saw movement of men and horses. Their pursuers were already halfway up the hill. Damn! They were only minutes behind! And as if in confirmation of this a bullet whined by his ear, followed a few seconds later by the crack of the shot and the noise of horses plunging through the undergrowth. He didn't know how many men were in the posse but there would be more than enough to be a match for him and Otis.

"We've gotta get out of here!" he yelled and leapt to his feet, reaching for his horse's reins.

"What about Elmer?"

"Iffen he can't get up and on his horse then he'll have to be left."

"Wilbur! You can't!" Elmer wailed. "They'll lynch me!"

"I don't know about this," Otis objected.

"Look I don't mean to let him be lynched but there ain't a whole lot we can do right now. He'll slow us down. We'll get caught too." Wilbur reached down to pat his brother's good shoulder. "Don't worry, Elmer, they won't hurt you. And we'll come back for you, I promise."

"Wilbur!"

"Get up then."

But Elmer couldn't. He was too scared, too hurt to even dare try.

"Come on, Otis, let's go! Now!"

Otis cast a look at Elmer, a look down the hill, and then a look at Wilbur. He didn't like any of this but Wilbur was probably right. Elmer was bad enough hurt that he wouldn't be able to ride quickly or for long, and they had no way of doctoring him, whereas surely a place like Rock Springs would have some sort of sawbones. It was probably best for Elmer if the posse took him back there. And he and Otis could save him later if they were still free. Besides he didn't want to be caught and put in prison.

With a little shrug he followed his brother to the horses.

"Come back! Wilbur! Otis!"

Elmer's panic-stricken voice followed his brothers as they rode swiftly over the top of the hill, out of the range of the posse's guns, but they took no notice.

★ ★ ★

"So this is Rock Springs," Lester Peabody said as he and Myra rode along the muddy street. "And it looks like Bennett was wrong and Tyler was telling the truth when he said he was a preacher."

"How do you know?"

"Look, up there." Peabody pointed up the hill to where the church was being built. "Come on, we'd better find the Marshal's office, so I can tell him why I'm here."

Myra nodded. She wished Mr Peabody wasn't going to arrest Jarrod Kilkline. He'd been a friend of the preacher who tried to help her. But from the few days she'd spent in his company she knew that Mr Peabody always did what he considered right and no matter what anyone argued he wouldn't take any notice. He was surely down on outlaws. "What are you going to tell the Marshal about me?"

"The truth, probably." Peabody's reply was as blunt as she'd feared it would be. "Don't worry, Myra. You haven't done anything wrong. He won't hurt you." Puzzled, he paused to look round. The streets were deserted and all the stores shut and locked up. "It's strange. No one seems to be around. I wonder where everyone is."

"Up there, see, Mr Peabody." Myra pointed to the end of the road. It was just possible to make out a large group of people gathered together.

"Let's go find out what's going on."
Now they were here Peabody wasn't
going to let the girl out of his sight in
case she took it into her head to warn
Kilkline of his presence.

As they got closer it was possible to
see that the citizens of Rock Springs
were all wearing various shades of dark
clothes. They stood in the middle of a
fenced off plot of land. The gate to it
was open and erected over the entrance
was a large wooden cross. All round
were other crosses marking burial sites.
It was an old, almost full cemetery, left
over from the mining days.

As they stopped outside the gate, a
woman in her forties, together with a
slightly older man, his face bruised
and cut, came over to them. Across
the crowd, Peabody could see a young
woman, head bowed, being held in the
arms of another woman; the preacher
standing close by. They were near a
closed coffin and he guessed the young
woman was the bereaved.

"That's Mr Tyler," Myra said.

"What's happened here?" Peabody asked the man.

"We had a robbery couple of days back. Three no goods tried to rob me." That explained the bruises. "Killed one of our citizens while they were at it. Shot the poor bastard in the back."

"Oh," said Myra. She glanced at Mr Peabody, wondering if Jarrod Kilkline was involved.

Peabody was wondering the same thing. He didn't think so. From all he'd learned of the young man, shooting someone in the back didn't seem to be his style.

"My husband, the Marshal, has taken a posse out after them," Naomi Cox went on. "We're hoping he'll be back any day now. Is there something we can do for you?"

"I'm looking for a man called Jarrod Kilkline." Peabody was aware of the young woman's startled, scared glance and wondered who she was. The preacher also looked up.

"Oh he's not here now," Naomi said.

Peabody saw the young woman put out a hand and the preacher step forward as if to stop Naomi from saying anything more. But before either of them could prevent her, Naomi went on. "He's out with the posse."

"I'll wait then."

17

"WELL, well, look here," Marshal Cox said as, at the head of the posse, he rode into the clearing and saw Elmer sitting up against a rock. "Left you to face the music on your own, have they, son?"

"Yeah," Elmer said sulkily. He looked thoroughly miserable and scared. And the scowls on the faces of his captors didn't exactly make him feel any happier. "Marshal," he added quickly, "it weren't me shot that man. I didn't even have my gun out."

"No," said Cox, "you were just one of the other two beating up on old Mr Hobson."

"You bastard!" A couple of the townsmen, friends of Mr Hobson, went up to Elmer, kicking him several times, making him scream in both pain and fright.

Cox let this go on for a little while before getting off his horse. "That's enough. Enough I said!" And he pulled them away, while Elmer lay where he was, curled up into a defensive ball. "Come on you," Cox said to him. "On your feet." He pulled roughly at Elmer's arm, making him yell again. But Cox was in no mood to be gentle. He didn't approve of cold blooded murder. He shook Elmer. "Where have the other two gone?"

"I dunno, mister," Elmer said, close to tears. "They rode off and left me here. How should I know where the bastards went."

"Don't you have a hideout or a meeting place?"

"No, sir. Honest."

"I don't believe him," Gus said. "We oughtta beat him up like he beat poor Mr Hobson. Make him talk."

"It's the truth! The truth!" Elmer cried, petrified. "I'd tell you iffen I

170

knew. I don't owe the bastards nothing. They left me behind!"

"Don't sniffle." Cox was experienced in handling prisoners. And he felt Elmer was telling the truth. No matter what they threatened him with he couldn't tell them something he didn't know.

"What are we going to do now, Marshal?" Jarrod asked. "We've got this one. But the other two, including the one who shot Parker, are still free. Are you going after them?"

"Umm, I don't know. This one's got a bad wound. Unless he gets medical attention he could die from it." Cox didn't mind his prisoners being threatened, even punched and kicked around some, but he didn't like them dying on him, if it could be prevented.

"We oughtta just string him up," Gus muttered.

Elmer moved a little closer to the Marshal. Why had he been the one shot? The one left behind? It wasn't fair.

"Now, now," Cox said. "We're meant to be improving ourselves, getting a church an' all. We've got to act right. Tell you what, Gus, why don't you and a couple of the others take this idiot back to Rock Springs? Me and the rest will continue on after the other two."

"All right."

Elmer thought the Deputy had a gleam in his eyes he didn't like much.

"And I want to hear that he got back in one piece."

"Yes, sir," Gus sighed.

"No shooting him because he tried to escape."

"I'll go with Gus, Marshal," Jarrod said. "I'd like to see how Ginny is."

"OK." That suited Cox, who wondered if Jarrod, who had admittedly taken no part in threatening or kicking Elmer, would be able to control himself so well when he came face to face with Parker's murderer.

It didn't suit Elmer. It was getting worse and worse as far as he was

172

concerned. "Please, Marshal, no," he begged. "They'll shoot me sure." But no one took any notice.

"Come on you." Gus pushed Elmer towards his horse. "Remember this, the Marshal ain't gonna be around. So you cause any trouble and I'll forget all about acting right and tie the noose round your neck myself!"

★ ★ ★

"Mr Tyler, what are we going to do?" Ginny asked, clinging to the preacher's jacket. "That awful man is going to arrest Jarrod and take him away. We've got to stop him."

"I don't see how." Tyler had taken her to the meadow where the half built church seemed to mock him for his once so high hopes. Hopes that were rapidly crumbling round him. "Mr Peabody is in the right, isn't he?"

"Yes," Ginny admitted. "But Jarrod hasn't done anything really bad. He doesn't deserve to go to prison. Isn't there some way of warning him?"

"Maybe. But I doubt it. Mr Peabody seems both determined and crafty. Don't underestimate him because he looks strange. He's followed Jarrod this far, all the way from Arizona. And if we do anything we might be the ones breaking the law."

"I don't care about that."

"Nor do I but I wouldn't put it past Peabody to arrest anyone, young woman or preacher, who got in his way."

"But I can't bear to think of Jarrod facing a trial and then being locked up in a cell. He's my older brother and he's always looked after me. All I can remember right now is us growing up together in Georgia and all the plans we had. None of this was meant to happen. It's not Jarrod's fault that our governments declared war, or that he lost the farm. He never meant to do anything wrong. He was desperate and led into it by a man called Harry Phillips."

"I'm sure that'll be taken into consideration."

"But supposing no one believes him?"

"Then I'll write a letter to go with Mr Peabody saying how Jarrod saved my life, testifying to his good character. That might help. If needs be I'll appear in court and speak up for him."

Ginny stared at him, tears making her eyes bright. "Would you really do that?"

"Yes." Tyler didn't add that he was doing it as much for Ginny as for Jarrod.

* * *

"Here you are, Mr Tyler," Naomi Cox handed the man a cup of coffee. He accepted it thankfully. "You've surely had a lot to deal with these past few days."

"You can say that again! I thought having my own church in my own town would make a pleasant change to riding

175

round California. I thought it would be quiet!"

"I hope you're not regretting coming here?"

"No, not really."

"How's Ginny?"

"Not so good."

"It's a real shame. Jarrod seemed such a nice young man, although Nigel was suspicious of him all along. Poor girl. It's not right that she's just lost her husband and now looks set to lose her brother as well. Isn't there anything we can do?" Naomi gave Tyler a sideways glance. She knew just as well as everyone else how he felt about Ginny, and while he might not be willing to help Jarrod, he would do all he could to help her.

"Jarrod is wanted by the law. There's no doubt of that. And I don't think your husband would or could stop that Peabody character from taking him in."

"Normally Nigel doesn't like or trust bounty hunters. He says they're just after the money."

"I agree but at least Peabody seems tough but fair. The warrant he's got for Jarrod says 'dead or alive' but unless Jarrod does anything stupid, I'm convinced Peabody will take him in alive."

"I hope so," Naomi said. "And, of course, we have another problem, don't we?"

"Myra?"

"Yes, Myra. She appeared to know you."

"In a way." And Tyler quickly went on to explain when and how he'd met the girl.

"Oh goodness, poor child! How awful. Of course, I suspected something of the sort. But to be betrayed by a relative she trusted at such a young age." Naomi shook her head. "We must do something for her." She was well known for supporting lost causes.

"She's certainly had a hard life and deserves some luck as what happened wasn't her fault. But I don't really see . . . "

"What about Mrs Goodman?"

"What about her?"

"She's always saying how she needs help at the boarding house. Wouldn't Myra be the ideal choice?"

Tyler frowned. "I don't know. Mrs Goodman is a God-fearing woman if ever there was one. Would she agree to, or approve of, having a whore, even a reformed one, living under her roof?"

"Need she know?"

"Mrs Goodman isn't stupid."

"Can't we think up a story to explain Myra's presence with Peabody? Surely in this case lying wouldn't be that great a sin if it helps the poor girl?"

"No I don't suppose it would." The two of them looked at one another and smiled. "Where's Myra now?"

"Mr Peabody left her with me. She's outside on the porch."

"Then why don't we put our heads together and think up this story? Then we can take her to see Mrs Goodman."

18

"WE shouldn't have left Elmer like that," Otis said. "He's our brother for Chrissakes."

"I don't like it any better than you. It was the only way. At least it's slowed the posse down. We're well ahead of them now."

"God, Wilbur, do you always just think of yourself?"

"Course I don't. What I meant was that it's given us the chance to decide what to do. And before you moan on at me any more what I mean by *that* is we've gotta decide how to rescue little Elmer."

"I don't understand." There didn't seem to be any problem to Otis.

Wilbur sighed. "We can't do anything rash. There are only two of us and a whole heap of them bastards. They'll be on their guard. We can't just ride

179

in and expect to ride out again without meeting resistance."

"Then what the hell do we do? He's our kin. We must do something."

Wilbur reached down to the knife he kept in his boot and held it out towards his brother so that its sharp blade glinted in the late evening sunlight. "Don't worry, Otis, I don't intend to let the good people of Rock Springs get away with shooting Elmer. He might be their prisoner right now but that won't be for long. I'll make 'em sorry right enough."

Otis grinned. That was what he liked to hear.

It was some time later when Wilbur suddenly said, "Hey, look." He pointed ahead to where the lights of a small hamlet twinkled in the darkened valley. "Let's see if the folks are friendly. We should at least be able to get fresh horses there." By which he meant steal rather than buy them.

Otis nodded thankfully. There might

also be the chance of some food and a good night's sleep.

They left their tired horses at the livery and equally tired and dispirited made their way towards the saloon.

And there found uproar.

Men were shouting at one another, almost coming to blows, while Bill Rogers, the bartender, tried to restore calm.

"We want the bastard who shot Ronny," someone yelled.

"And I want Myra back . . . "

"We don't care about her."

" . . . but yelling and arguing amongst ourselves ain't going to do either. We've gotta make plans."

"What the hell's going on?" Wilbur demanded and as the men realized they had two strangers in their midst the uproar died down and they fell silent, staring at the two brothers in suspicious anger.

"I could ask you the same," Rogers said. "Who are you? Why are you both so lathered up?"

"It's a long story. We got into some trouble."

"Hey, Wilbur, don't tell 'em," Otis said in some alarm. But Wilbur could recognize badmen like himself and knew that the men here represented no threat. "A robbery went wrong. Our brother was shot and he's now a prisoner."

"Yeah." Otis glared at his brother.

"Where was this?" Rogers asked.

"In Rock Springs."

"Christ," someone else said, "everything's happening at Rock Springs these days."

"What d'you mean?"

"Only that we've had several people through here last couple of weeks all on their way there."

"Yeah and one of 'em shot and killed our friend."

Rogers wasn't all that concerned about Ronnie Bennett's demise. As far as he was concerned the man was a bully and had brought it on himself. He was concerned about Myra, who had been popular and made him a lot of money. "And he took one of my whores with him. Whether she went willingly or was forced remains to be seen. I want her back."

Bennett's friends weren't all that concerned about Myra. They'd been too scared of Ronnie to pay for her services. "And we want the bastard done for Ronnie."

"And we want Elmer," said Otis.

"But Rock Springs has law, plenty of it too," Rogers pointed out. "I keep telling you all we can't just shoot our way in and out."

"That's what Wilbur says."

Wilbur's eyes had lit up in thought. He suddenly grinned. Here, surely, was the chance not only to rescue Elmer and take revenge on those sonsofbitches who'd shot him but also at last to get his hands on the church money.

"I reckon we all owe Rock Springs something. It's probably hiding your whore and your friend's killer. Now it's got our brother. There's also money there for the taking. How about we join forces? Show 'em all they can't mess with us and get away with it?"

Things could hardly have worked out better!

19

"**P**OSSE'S coming in, posse's coming in!" Outside someone rode up and down yelling out the news. "They've got one of the murdering bastards with 'em!"

Tyler leapt to his feet. "We'd better go see."

Peabody also got up. "I'll stand for no interference from any of you," he said, aware of the scowls of Tyler, Ginny, Mrs Goodman and Myra. He wasn't the most popular man in town, or at the boarding house, but that hardly bothered him. He was used to standing alone.

"Ginny, you'd better stay here."

"No, Mr Tyler, I'm coming."

Despite the late hour they weren't the only ones making their way to the Marshal's office. By the time they got there quite a crowd had gathered. At the far end of the road they could see the approach of several riders.

"It's not the whole posse," Tyler said.

"Is Jarrod with them?" Ginny stood on tiptoe to see over people's heads.

"I can't see . . . yes there he is."

"Where's Peabody? What's he up to?" Ginny caught hold of the preacher's hand, holding it tightly.

"He seems to have disappeared. Maybe, if we can get close enough for Jarrod to see us and for us to make ourselves heard, we can warn him before Peabody can do anything. Come on, let's try." Tyler put his arm round Ginny's waist, pulling her close to him, as he tried to force a way through to the front.

Mrs Goodman followed on behind but Myra, unsure of herself and her position in the town, remained where she was.

Boos and jeers were now ringing out as the crowd spotted the subdued young man riding between Gus and

Jarrod. If anyone noticed the bruises on his face they weren't about to say so.

Tyler hoped there wouldn't be any trouble. He couldn't cope with Jarrod, Peabody, Ginny and a lynch mob!

"Jarrod! Jarrod! Be careful!" Ginny called. But she and Tyler were still lost amongst the angry and excited crowd, and, to her dismay, she realized that Jarrod couldn't hear her above the shouts and calls.

The small group of men came to a halt outside the office. Gus dismounted, pulling Elmer off his horse. Jarrod followed while the others got ready to go home, their part in the proceedings over. Gus took his prisoner's arm pushing him towards the door. The crowd surged forward and Ginny almost fell, so that Tyler was occupied with helping her. Gus came to a halt, Jarrod by his side.

"There'll be no trouble here," he shouted. "This man has done wrong but he'll get a fair trial."

More jeers followed this statement. "Yeah and then he'll hang!"

"Where's my husband?" Naomi Cox called.

"He's all right, Mrs Cox. He's taken the rest of the men to continue after the other two who got away when this one was shot. We didn't run into any trouble. OK, folks, you can go home now. Excitement's over." To Gus's annoyance no one took any notice. He looked round them all and seeing the person he sought added, "Mr Hobson, is that you? Can you use your doctoring skills to see to the sonofabitch's wound?"

"Umm, I suppose so." Mr Hobson sounded most reluctant.

"Best to go home, folks," Gus said again, hoping they would do so. "Come on, Jarrod, let's get this bastard locked up and the door secured."

"Jarrod!" Ginny screamed.

Again he didn't hear but turned into the Marshal's office. And came to a startled, scared halt.

Just inside the door, Lester Peabody stood facing him, gun in hand.

Jarrod recognized him at once. "Oh God," he muttered. His hand went to his gun but he knew resistance was useless. The other man's gun was already pointed at him, and he looked as if he wouldn't hesitate to use it.

"What's going on here?" Gus demanded, pushing Elmer further into the room.

Peabody shoved the gunbarrel against Jarrod's chest. "You're under arrest. You going to give me any trouble?"

"No, sir."

"Good."

"I said what's going on?"

"This." Peabody reached into his coat pocket and drew out a Wanted poster, which he flung down on the desk.

Jarrod was aware of Gus's look of surprise. Then the door opened and Tyler and Ginny, together with Naomi Cox and Mrs Goodman all pushed their way inside. He wished they weren't here. He didn't want them to see his humiliation.

"Jarrod," Ginny said, with a little sob.

"Mr Kilkline is my prisoner." Peabody sounded as if he too didn't want all these witnesses. Even so their presence didn't stop him doing what he did next. He suddenly hit Jarrod hard in the stomach.

All the breath left Jarrod's body in a painful whoosh. Gasping he collapsed to his knees.

"Hey now!" Tyler protested while both Ginny and Mrs Cox cried out.

"Sir!" Gus said angrily.

"It's all right, gents, ladies, there's no need for any of you to look so worried. I don't usually ill treat my prisoners unless they ask for it but that was one I owed him." Peabody holstered his gun and catching Jarrod by his coat collar pulled him up. "Deputy, I think you should put your two prisoners in the cells." And he shoved Jarrod forward, hard.

"Stop it!" Ginny cried and would have gone to her brother's aid had not Tyler held her back. "Can't one of you do something?"

"I don't understand this," Gus said, bewildered.

"You don't need to, Deputy. You just need to do your duty and lock the pair of them up." Peabody gave Jarrod another shove.

"You don't have to be so rough," Jarrod managed to say, even though he was still short of breath. For such a slight man, Peabody sure packed a punch. "I'm sorry for hitting you but you'd have done the same."

"I just want you to know who's boss. You've led me a pretty dance over the last couple of months and I don't mind admitting I'm fed up with you."

"Gave you the runaround didn't I?"

"Yes but I knew I'd catch up sooner or later."

Gus scooped up the keys to the cells from the Marshal's desk and led Elmer towards the door at the rear of the office. Elmer recognized Tyler, and puzzled as to why he wasn't dead but thinking even more trouble was about to be heaped upon his unwilling head, said to him, "It was all a misunderstanding. We didn't mean to rob you."

"Nor to leave me for dead I suppose? Ah, here is Mr Hobson with his doctor's bag."

"What happens now?" Jarrod asked Peabody.

"We set out for Arizona tomorrow. How we get there depends on you."

"I said I wouldn't give you any trouble. And I won't."

"I know."

Jarrod allowed the small man to push and prod him forward. He glanced once at Ginny but there was no chance for any words between them. In the cell block, he was pushed into one cell, Elmer into the other.

"Can I leave Mr Kilkline safely in your hands, Deputy?"

Gus's eyes narrowed at the implied

192

criticism. "I won't let him escape if that's what you're afraid of."

"Good. I'll come by and collect him tomorrow morning."

"Perhaps you ought to wait until the Marshal gets back."

Peabody shrugged. "That won't be necessary, Deputy. I'll see you tomorrow." And tipping his hat to Jarrod he left them.

At the same time, Mr Hobson went into Elmer's cell. "Take your shirt off, son. Now let's have a look at you." He began to poke and prod at the wound, making Elmer cry out.

"He's hurting me real bad on purpose," he moaned. "Don't I get anything to deaden the pain? What about some whiskey?"

"No," said Gus. "Nothing."

Elmer suddenly gave a shrill scream. He spent the next few minutes hollering and begging for mercy.

Gus went over to where Jarrod was sitting on the bunk, his head in his hands. "I'm sorry, Jarrod, what else

can I do but keep you locked up?"
He scowled. It was all very well being
a deputy but this was beyond him and
he wished Marshal Cox was here to
take charge.

"It ain't your fault. Gus."

"Yeah?"

"Don't let Ginny see me in here.
Please."

"I'll do my best to keep her out."

"Deputy," Mr Hobson called Gus
over to him. "The bullet is out. It
looked worse than it actually was."

"He surely made enough noise about
it."

"He'll be all right so long as the
wound is kept clean and the bandages
changed twice a day."

The two men went out and Elmer
looked at Jarrod. "Are we goin' to be
lynched?"

"I'm not, you might be. Gus isn't
very experienced at being a lawman
and rather than protect you he might
decide to let his fellow citizens in. But
they haven't got any beef with me."

"Oh God. Oh please I don't wanna die."

"You should have thought of that before. Now shut up and leave me be. I've got problems enough of my own without bothering about yours." And Jarrod lay back on the bunk, pulling the blanket up over him.

He felt wretched. He'd known all along that his dream of becoming a farmer again was just that, a dream, but he still had allowed himself, deep inside, a little hope. All that was dashed now.

20

"HEY, deputy, I can't eat this slop!" Elmer Jackson was awake and whining.

The night had passed peacefully with the citizens going home once they realized Gus was going to stand guard all night. They had no desire to get shot, or shoot Gus, in trying to lynch Elmer. What was the point? The judge would sentence him to hang and they could wait till then.

Now that his wound had been seen to and was no longer hurting and he wasn't afraid of being lynched, Elmer had decided to make a nuisance of himself. "When am I goin' to get something decent to eat? You can't treat me like this!"

"Shut your mouth!" Gus was rapidly becoming irritated with the young man. He was a deputy, paid to uphold the law. He wasn't paid to act as servant to a prisoner, especially one charged with robbery, violence and murder. "I should make the most of it," he added nastily. "Once the judge sentences you to the gallows, you won't have much time left to eat."

Elmer lumbered to his feet and stuck his face close to the bars of the cell. "Think yourself so brave don't you? You won't be so brave when my brothers come calling."

"Oh yeah? I don't see 'em riding down the street. They left you alone, Elmer, remember? I wouldn't hold out too much hope. I reckon they'll leave you to rot."

"They won't leave me," Elmer screamed. "They'll be here soon."

"But quite probably not soon enough."

Gus grinned annoyingly and left the cells. He knew he shouldn't torment the prisoner. Marshal Cox wouldn't like it if he found out. But Elmer deserved it for what he'd done. Besides most of the other people who'd occupied the Rock

Springs jail cells since Gus became a deputy, were Saturday night drunks caught fighting one another or shooting at the moon. Now he had two real desperadoes behind bars. And they were both proving to be a disappointment.

Jarrod just sat there on his bunk, saying nothing. And as for Elmer, well real outlaws were meant to be glamorous and exciting. They weren't meant to complain about their breakfast.

★ ★ ★

Once Gus had gone, Elmer turned from the bars and looked across at Jarrod. He was puzzled. Hadn't Jarrod been part of the posse that captured him? Yet now here he was in the next cell. It didn't make sense to Elmer. But as Jarrod was eating the same slop as him there couldn't be that much of a mistake. Jarrod was also a prisoner.

"So, what they got you for?"

"Robbery and murder," Jarrod replied. He sat with his back to Elmer, hoping the young man would take the hint that he didn't want to talk.

But Elmer's eyes had widened. A robber and murderer! Goodness that was as bad as Wilbur! Worse really. Wilbur might be a robber but he was a murderer only by mistake. "That's what they've got me for too," he boasted as if Jarrod didn't know anything about him. "But I shan't be here for long."

"Why? Do you expect them to hang you or let you go?"

Elmer didn't know whether that was a joke or not but he laughed anyway, a bit nervously. "Now, course not. Like I told that fool deputy my brothers are coming to break me out."

"Really?"

"Yeah, really. Say, you can come with us if you like."

Jarrod wasn't sure which would be worse. Going back to Arizona with Lester Peabody or being rescued by the backshooters of his brother-in-law. "Let's wait till it happens."

"Oh it'll happen," Elmer said, hoping

that it would. For all he knew Wilbur and Otis were on their way back to California. The bastards.

★ ★ ★

Marshal Cox led the posse down a steep slope of rocks and thorny bushes. At the bottom a fast running stream cut across the middle of a brush choked meadow. Without Gus to do the tracking, following the trail hadn't been nearly so easy and the two remaining Jacksons were now several hours ahead. But he couldn't have kept Gus with him, a lawman had had to accompany Elmer Jackson back to Rock Springs. Neither could he have gone back and left Gus out here on his own, facing the two still armed and more dangerous outlaws.

But the result was . . .

"We've lost the trail, boys." He came to a halt, pushing his hat to the back of his head and scratching his forehead.

"We'll ride on for a while longer but it don't look good."

A couple of hours later one of the possemen came riding back, face red with excited urgency. "Sir! Marshal!"

"What is it?"

"I've found the trail again. Over there," he pointed to the far slope of the hill. "But, Marshal, there are six riders now."

"What? Are you sure?"

"Yeah."

"I meant are you sure it's the Jacksons?"

"Yessir. There's that mark on the front right hoof of one of the horses that's unmistakable. It's them all right. And they've got four others with 'em."

God only knew where they had come from, Cox thought, but worse was to follow.

"And, Marshal, it looks like they're heading back to Rock Springs!"

All the men looked at one another.

"They're going to rescue Elmer," Cox said. And Gus was back there, on his own. "Let's get going," he added urgently, but with the dreadful knowledge that they would be too late.

★ ★ ★

Mrs Goodman had a good idea about what Myra really was. Oh, Mr Tyler and Naomi Cox had spun her some line about how the girl had been found in the mountains following an accident to the family wagon, but Mrs Goodman could see through that. For one thing there was the matter of the girl's clothes, or rather her lack of them. She didn't even have a change of underwear! And there was her way of talking.

But Mrs Goodman wasn't as fierce and unforgiving as she sometimes pretended. Myra was only fifteen. Still a child in some ways. Besides if Mr Tyler, a preacher, was willing to lie for her then surely it was Mrs Goodman's Christian duty to help her, to take her in and teach her how to behave properly. And the way to do that was through hard work, of which there was plenty at the boarding house.

Besides having a prostitute — there she had admitted the word — under her roof wasn't so bad considering some of the people she'd boarded lately. What with Mr Kilkline being a stagecoach robber, and now there was the very strange Mr Peabody, who was a bounty hunter.

It was enough to make her feel quite faint.

However it wasn't quite bad enough to prevent her making breakfast for all those people at the jail. Far better her food than that served up by the cafe. Mrs Goodman knew her duty as a good citizen of Rock Springs.

She went into the dining room where Myra was laying the table.

"Myra, take this food to the Marshal's office." Mrs Goodman handed her a large basket. "Young Mr Wilkinson," she noticed the way Myra blushed at mention of Gus's name, "has stayed there all night guarding the prisoners and even if they can put up with those awful cafe meals I don't see why he should. Go on, quickly now."

"All right, Mrs Goodman."

Myra felt quite nervous at the thought of seeing the young deputy again. She had seen him last night as he escorted his prisoner into the jail house. He had been so brave, standing up to the crowd. He was good looking too. Even if her knowledge of men had been gained reluctantly, she knew enough to realize that Gus was completely different from the men who had come to the saloon. He looked nice and would never hurt her.

★ ★ ★

Lester Peabody got up, dressing carefully, parting his hair and smoothing it back. As long as the weather remained fine it shouldn't take long for him to return Mr Kilkline to Tucson. Then he could go after Harry Phillips. Unfortunately his trail would be cold by now. He could be anywhere. But Peabody had the time and patience to search for him.

He shrugged into his coat. Thank God this assignment would soon be over. It had proved tougher than most but it wouldn't be long now . . .

★ ★ ★

"Please, Mr Tyler, I must see Jarrod," Ginny begged. "Take me with you."

"He asked not to see you."

"That's only because he feels ashamed. He's no need to. I'm his sister. I must see him. Please."

Tyler held her hands for a moment. "I'll ask him. If he doesn't want to then you have no choice but to accept that. However hard this is for you, it's much harder for him."

★ ★ ★

"So that's Rock Springs is it?" Bill Rogers said.

The Jacksons, Rogers and the three of Ronnie Bennett's friends who had come to revenge the dead man, came to a halt up in the hills where they could look down at the town. They had ridden long and hard to reach their destination so quickly because Wilbur wanted to get to Rock Springs while the Marshal and the posse were still out looking for him and Otis and all they had to deal with was the deputy.

Wilbur grinned. "Yeah. And there's the church. Damn fine ain't it? Pity the good citizens won't have the money to finish it."

"What we gonna do, Wilbur?" Otis asked.

"We ride on down, rescue Elmer and steal the money!" Wilbur reached over to pat his brother's back. "It won't be difficult."

"Don't forget, I want Myra back," Rogers said. "Alive and well."

"And we want that damn Eastern greenhorn."

"All right. You'll all get what you want. With our help." And Wilbur dug his spurs into his horse's side, sending it into a gallop.

21

GUS went very red when he saw Myra coming through the door. Rock Springs didn't provide him with any companionship in the form of young women of his own age. He'd spotted the girl amongst the crowd the night before and later Reverend Tyler, keeping him company at the jailhouse, had explained who she was. Gus was about the only one willing to believe the respectable version of Myra's past.

He'd immediately liked the look of her but having no idea of what to say or how to behave, hoped he wouldn't meet her. Now here she was coming into the jailhouse!

Gus might be shy and awkward, he was also a polite young man. And Myra was carrying a large basket. Springing up and saying, "Here let me," he took it from her.

Somewhat to her own surprise Myra found herself awkward in his company as well. Keeping her eyes lowered to the floor, she said, "Mrs Goodman sent over food for you and the prisoners."

"Oh good." Like Elmer, Gus didn't like the cafe meals.

For a moment the two youngsters stood in silence, not looking at one another, not knowing what to say.

"I suppose I'd better go back. Mrs Goodman will want help with the breakfast dishes."

Gus gathered together all his courage and gulping, said, "Perhaps I can see you later."

"I'd like that," Myra smiled.

She turned towards the door just as it slammed open and Wilbur and Otis Jackson pushed their way in. She gave a cry of terror as she saw Bill Rogers and three of Ronnie's friends.

"Jesus!" Gus exclaimed as scared as Myra. He paused, not knowing what to do, whether to put up his hands in surrender or make a fight of it by going for his guns — but it was already too late.

Wilbur shoved Myra aside, causing the girl to bang against the wall, and clouted Gus round the ear with the barrel of his gun.

Vaguely Gus heard Myra scream again. Everything swam round in front of him and his legs wobbled. He would have fallen had Wilbur not grabbed his arm supporting him.

"Bastard," Wilbur snarled. "Where's Elmer?"

In a voice that didn't sound like his own, Gus mumbled, "Through there, in the cells."

"Get the keys," Wilbur ordered and pushed Gus behind the desk. "Hurry it up."

Meanwhile Bill Rogers had caught hold of Myra. "My, my, this is a piece of luck. Look who we've got here, boys."

"Leave me alone," Myra said, so scared she began to cry.

"And all dressed up in fancy duds. Never mind, we'll soon have them off you."

"Leave her be," Gus echoed Myra's cry. Then Wilbur hit him with the gun again, this time in the back, and flung him towards the door to the cells. Flanked by the two Jacksons, Gus had to let Elmer out. And what would happen then?

"Where's the bastard you went off with?" One of Bennett's friends asked Myra.

"I . . . I don't know. He ain't here any more."

"Did you go willingly?" Rogers asked. "Or was you forced?"

"He kidnapped me," Myra was wise enough to lie.

"Umm, we'll soon see about that."

"It's the truth. He made me go with him. I didn't want to."

"Someone let him out of the cellar."

"Well it wasn't me. Why would I have wanted to leave you, Mr Rogers?"

The man laughed. "You've got spunk

I'll give you that."

"What I want to know is, where's the bastard now?"

"He's not here," Myra repeated but she had a feeling they didn't believe her about that either.

Jarrod and Elmer had heard the commotion in the office. They stared at the door.

"What the hell is going on?"

"Dunno," Elmer began before the door opened and Gus was shoved through so hard he sprawled on the floor. "Wilbur! Otis!" he shouted. "See," he told Gus who was just picking himself up. "See, I told you my brothers wouldn't let me rot here. Hey, Wilbur, that damnfool deputy talked to me real bad."

"He did, did he?" Otis aimed a kick at Gus. "Hey, who's this?" he added as he saw Jarrod.

"He's a robber and a murderer," Elmer said proudly as if sharing the cells with such a person gave him added status. "I promised when you came you'd let him out and he could come with us."

"Sure, why not?" Wilbur unlocked both cells.

Jarrod stood there for a moment, wondering what to do. He didn't want to go with these three. Backshooters, robbers. Parker's murderers. He'd rather stay behind and be taken back to Arizona, and prison. He was frightened, wondering what would happen if Wilbur Jackson recognized him as a member of the posse, and angry, wanting to punish them for Ginny's grief.

But he wasn't left with much choice as Otis bundled him through the door. Behind him he could hear Gus being punched and kicked by Wilbur and Elmer. Supposing they shot the young deputy? It was quite likely they would. What was he going to do then? What could he do? They were the ones with the guns.

And things went from bad to considerable worse when he saw the other four men in the office. One he recognized as the bartender from Ronnie Bennett's saloon. And there in their midst, alone and frightened, was Myra.

★ ★ ★

Brian Tyler left the boarding house just before Peabody. He was determined to get to the jailhouse first, not only to see Jarrod but to make sure Peabody didn't have a chance to hit the young man again. He also wanted to prevent Peabody leaving before he had the chance to talk Jarrod into seeing Ginny.

He was almost at the jailhouse when he noticed six horses tied up at the hitching rail across the road outside the general store. Bit unusual that but he had no more time to wonder about it as a shot came from the jailhouse. Followed by a scream. And several more shots.

He broke into a run.

★ ★ ★

214

"Come on let's go," Rogers said.

"What about the money?" Otis asked. "We ain't going without that."

"Do what you want. I've got what I came for," Rogers squeezed Myra's arm.

"What about the greenhorn?"

"We can't search the whole town for him."

"Hey now . . . " Bennett's friend protested.

"We can't take Peabody here, there are too many people around. We'll have to lay in wait for him somewhere outside town, after we've dealt with the girl. Come on," and Rogers began to drag Myra towards the door.

"No!" she screamed.

"No!" said Gus and pulled away from Wilbur's grip to fling himself at Rogers and Myra. They all went down in a heap. Somehow Gus managed to roll on top of Myra. At the same time he drew one of his guns, which Wilbur had foolishly not taken from him. He fired.

He didn't hit Rogers but the bullet struck one of the men behind him in the leg. The man screamed and fell to the floor.

Gus tried to pull Myra out of the way and at the same time, Rogers, Wilbur and Otis all shot at him.

Myra screamed again as one of the bullets ploughed into Gus's chest. Losing his grip on his gun, the young man collapsed back on top of the girl, blood beginning to run down his shirt.

Jarrod quickly ducked down behind the Marshal's desk out of the way.

Rogers dashed forward making a grab at Myra but he quickly gave up on that idea. Wilbur and Otis were still shooting at Gus and Rogers was in danger of getting in the way. Myra wasn't worth getting shot for. Plenty of other whores where she came from. "Let's go!" he yelled.

Elmer caught hold of Wilbur's arm. "The Deputy's dead! Come on!"

"The money."

"Damn that." Elmer just wanted to get away.

* * *

Tyler reached the door to the office just as it opened and three men raced out. They knocked into him and he went flying backwards. Close behind them were the Jackson brothers. Tyler just had time to roll out of the way as Wilbur and Otis both fired at him. They were followed by a fourth stranger with a leg wound.

Tyler scrambled forward, grabbing him round the waist, wrestling him to the ground. "No you don't!" he said, clinging on to him, even though the man kicked and fought. From where he lay he could look into the jailhouse. "Oh God," he whispered as he saw Myra bending over Gus, holding him on her lap.

Jarrod was also bent over Gus, hefting his second gun from its holster.

"Jarrod, no!" Tyler said thinking that

the young man was going to join the Jacksons.

* * *

Lester Peabody hadn't been far behind Tyler. He too heard the firing and saw the men erupt from the jailhouse. He didn't hesitate. Standing still in the middle of the sidewalk, he drew the Colt 45 from his shoulder holster and carefully aimed. His shot hit another of Bennett's friends in the back. The man collapsed in the street and Otis almost fell over him.

Firing as he went, Peabody ran down the road and got to the jailhouse just as Jarrod rushed out. He brought up his gun.

"No! No! I'm with you!" Jarrod yelled and began to fire at the men across the way.

22

AS Wilbur, Otis and Bill Rogers all stopped to return the fire, Peabody skidded to a halt, diving behind a horse trough.

"Get down!" he yelled at Jarrod.

And Jarrod flung himself to the ground, while several bullets broke the glass in the jailhouse windows behind him.

At the same time Mr Hobson emerged from the real estate office. He held a rifle and began to fire it. It didn't appear as if he would actually hit anything but at least he helped to keep the men pinned down.

Wilbur Jackson couldn't believe it — everything was going wrong; yet again. All right Elmer had been rescued and the damnfool deputy shot but they hadn't got the church money. They'd lost Myra. And they hadn't killed the

Eastern greenhorn. From the glimpse he had of the man shooting at them that was probably him across the way — although there was certainly nothing greenhornish about the way he was behaving.

And where the hell had that damn preacher come from? How the hell had he got here?

Now they were being shot at from all sides.

Elmer went to get on his horse and Wilbur stopped him. "Don't be a fool."

"Let me go," Elmer begged, terrified. "Please."

"You'll be an easy target up there!"

"Can't we make a run for it?" Otis said. "There's only three of 'em against us."

As far as Wilbur was concerned that was three too many but at the same time they had to do something. They couldn't remain here in the middle of the street. Other citizens would soon arrive to join in the excitement. They'd be trapped.

* * *

Heaving the wounded man after him, Tyler made it into the Marshal's office, kicking the door shut behind him. Pushing the man aside and taking his gun, he went over to where Myra crouched over Gus.

"He's dead," she wailed.

"No, he's not." Gus was breathing very shallowly but he was at least breathing. "But he soon will be if we don't stop the bleeding." Tyler tore Gus's bloody shirt pulling it aside, revealing the bullet wound, from which blood still pumped. The bullet was embedded in his chest but he couldn't do anything about that. "Myra, dear, don't take this the wrong way but are you wearing a petticoat?"

"Yes."

"Then perhaps you'd be so kind as to take it off and tear it into strips for bandages."

Blushing, although she didn't know why, Myra stood up. She turned her back, hitched up her skirt and wriggled out of the petticoat Mrs Goodman had given her. When she turned back, it was to see that the preacher had taken off his own coat and used it as a pillow for Gus's head.

"Hurry, girl."

And with trembling hands Myra tore the petticoat into long strips. Tyler took one piece and folding it up into a pad placed it over the wound, the rest he used to tie it tightly into position. Gus moaned once or twice, his eyelids fluttered, otherwise he made no sound or gave any indication that he was alive. Tyler sat back on his heels. "That's all I can do just now."

"Is he going to be all right?"

"I don't know. That's in the hands of God and Gus himself. Perhaps with your help . . . "

"I won't leave him," Myra promised.

Tyler patted her shoulder then went over to the other wounded man. "Oh don't worry," he said as the man gave him a scared look. "I'm not about to shoot you, although I should for all the trouble you've helped cause."

"I'm unarmed, I'm wounded . . . "

"Shut up and get up or I will shoot you."

Groaning and sniffling the man got to his feet and Tyler shoved him through to the cells, locking him in. At least he would cause no more trouble.

* * *

Wilbur made up his mind. "Keep firing at the bastards. Let's get outta here!"

Elmer needed no more urging. He flung himself up into the saddle, hands flapping at the reins, and bending low over his horse's back, spurred it forward.

Bill Rogers did likewise. But as he rode down the street, Mr Hobson stepped out of his office doorway. He fired, missed, then as Rogers rode by smashed the rifle hard into his chest, sending him flying backwards off his horse. The wind knocked out of him, Rogers landed with a thump but still managed to bring up and fire his gun. The bullet caught Mr Hobson in the arm and he dropped the rifle, reeling back to sit in his doorway, a stunned expression on his face.

Rogers scrambled to his feet only to see Jarrod getting up from where he had been crouching on the sidewalk. Rogers raised his gun and Jarrod shot him, twice, once in the head, the other in the throat.

Meanwhile Ronnie Bennett's third friend took advantage of the confusion to ride away in the other direction. Neither Peabody nor Jarrod took much notice. The man was out of the fight, out of the town and probably out of the Rockies as well!

Wilbur and Otis weren't so lucky in their attempted getaway.

Made nervous by all the firing and shouting, the remaining horses milled round nervously. One galloped, riderless, down the street.

Otis couldn't get his foot in the stirrup and, cursing, gave up trying. And as Wilbur tried to mount his animal, it shied away from him. Somehow he caught hold of another horse's bridle, managing to keep it between him and Otis and the jailhouse, while shooting at Jarrod and Peabody under the horse's neck.

Peabody ducked behind the horse trough again as the jailhouse door opened behind him and Tyler stood there, joining in with the firing. Peabody was as much surprised as anyone about a preacher who was prepared to kill people but he wasn't going to argue with it. Tyler could help Kilkline because if he didn't do something, and quick, the other bastard, Elmer Jackson, would get away.

Keeping low Peabody ran across the road to the horses. He dragged the reins out of Wilbur's hands and leapt up into the saddle. Wilbur tried to stop him and Peabody kicked out, his shoe catching the man on the jaw.

"He's real determined ain't he?" Jarrod said to no one in particular, reluctant admiration in his voice.

Most of their cover had gone and Wilbur knew he and Otis couldn't remain where they were.

"The real estate office," he yelled because that was the only place open. Pushing and pulling his brother along he fled across the road. He kicked Mr Hobson's body aside and they dived inside.

"Now what?" Tyler asked, going up to Jarrod.

"They can't stay in there forever. We can wait 'em out."

"I'm going to help Mr Hobson."

"You can't. They'll shoot you."

"We can't leave him there, hurt like he is. You cover me, Jarrod."

As Tyler reached Mr Hobson, glad to see he was conscious and didn't look badly hurt, the door opened. Otis appeared on the other side. He shot at Tyler but somehow even at that close range the bullet missed. Tyler came upright and raised his gun. He didn't miss. With a surprised look on his face, Otis tumbled to the floor.

From somewhere beyond, Tyler heard Mrs Hobson scream. He ran through the office into the house at the rear. The woman was lying on the floor, a gash on her forehead.

She raised a shaking hand. "He went through there."

Tyler saw her pointing at an open window. Saying "Stay here," he ran back outside. "Jarrod, be careful. Wilbur's got out."

★ ★ ★

Peabody caught up with Elmer on the road that led up from the creek into the foothills. As he heard the other horse, Elmer looked round and Peabody saw the panic on the young man's face as he realized it wasn't his brothers following him. Several times

Elmer turned in the saddle to fire but Peabody ducked and the bullets came nowhere near. Peabody didn't bother to shoot back, he had no intention of wasting his ammunition.

For a while the road twisted and turned upwards, following the line of the creek, until it came to a long, straight stretch.

Peabody stopped and took the rifle from its scabbard. He was glad to see that it was fairly new and looked like it was kept in reasonable condition. He raised it to his shoulder and fired, hoping the sights were set right.

Evidently they weren't because while he was aiming at Elmer, he was dismayed to see he'd shot the horse instead. Squealing the animal went down on its haunches and Elmer tumbled over its neck and bounced on the road.

By the time Peabody got there, Elmer was struggling to sit up. Peabody grinned and said, "Come on, son."

Elmer raised an unhappy face towards

his pursuer. "Don't shoot, please," he whispered. He'd had quite enough excitement for a while and didn't want any more; he'd take his chances with judge and jury.

* * *

"What's happening?" Ginny cried as she, Naomi Cox and Mrs Goodman hurried down the street towards the jailhouse. All three came to a startled halt, hardly able to believe their eyes. All round was utter chaos.

Mr Hobson was being helped towards the jailhouse by Brian Tyler, who had a gun in one hand; Mrs Hobson had emerged from the real estate office, a bruise on her face; a dead body lay in the doorway, another in the street; a couple of horses milled around.

Other armed townsmen were arriving on the scene.

"It's all right," Tyler called. "The Jacksons were here."

"Oh God," Naomi Cox said. "Is Mr Hobson badly hurt?"

"No, but Gus is. He was beaten and shot."

"Is Myra all right?" Mrs Goodman asked, aware that she had sent the girl to the jailhouse.

"She's with him now."

"Where's Jarrod?" asked Ginny, staring wildly round her.

Tyler handed Mr Hobson over to Naomi Cox and went up to the girl. "He's gone after Wilbur Jackson."

"I must go find him."

"No," he caught her arm stopping her. "Jarrod has been a soldier. He's aware of the dangers and will be careful. He doesn't want to have to worry about you."

Ginny didn't like it, but she knew the preacher was right. "Is there anything I can do here?"

Tyler admired her bravery. "You can help with Gus."

★ ★ ★

Making sure his gun was loaded, Jarrod started down the street, keeping close to the shadows of the buildings. If Wilbur Jackson had any sense, he would head for the livery stable and hope to steal a horse there. Of course, Wilbur might not have any sense at all but Jarrod went in that direction anyway. He didn't know if Tyler was around or if he'd stayed with the Hobsons. He couldn't see or hear him.

Jarrod was aware of his heart beating wildly. It wasn't just as the result of the fight back at the jailhouse. Here he was, probably alone, stalking the man who had shot Parker in the back, and who, with nothing to lose, wouldn't hesitate to kill again. But Jarrod was determined that, if he had anything to do with it, Wilbur wouldn't get away.

There was movement ahead. Jarrod came to a halt. Nothing. Perhaps it was his imagination.

He crept on towards the stables. And as he came to an alleyway between two of the deserted saloons, Wilbur stepped out of the blackness and shot at him. The bullet grazed Jarrod's arm and surprised, he almost tripped over.

Quickly he scuttled out of the way, getting his back up against one of the saloons. No more sound. Wilbur didn't follow up his advantage, probably his only thought was to get away.

Cautiously Jarrod went down the alley and out at the other end, finding himself near the back of the stables.

And there was Wilbur, just about to go into the yard.

"Stop right there you sonofabitch!" Jarrod yelled.

The man flung himself round and started firing.

Jarrod brought his own gun up and marched forward, getting closer to Wilbur all the time, shooting back. Somewhere deep inside he knew he was taking chances but all he could see was Parker's dead body and Ginny's grief. And here was the bastard responsible! It was going to end here, one way or the other.

"This is for my sister."

The force of the bullet as it struck Wilbur lifted him up and deposited him on his back in the dirt.

As Jarrod reached him, Wilbur squinted up at him. "Me and my brothers never did have much luck," he said and then he died.

23

GUS WILKINSON slowly blinked open his eyes. He couldn't understand where he was. He didn't recognize the room and it was dark. He didn't understand why his chest hurt or why he felt so weak. Amongst all his aches and pains, he realized that one of his hands was being held between two others that were cool and dry. He raised his eyes and saw someone sitting in the shadows by the bedside.

"What . . . where?" he managed to say and tried, unsuccessfully, to raise his head.

"Hush, hush. You're in a room at Mrs Goodman's." Myra reached forward to wipe his forehead. "Don't move. You were shot . . . "

"The Jacksons!" Gus tried again to get up.

Myra pushed him back. "It's all right. They're all either dead or in prison. Mr Tyler, Jarrod and that horrid Mr Peabody saw to that. And Marshal Cox has just got back with the posse. He's busy taking statements. He's put in a request that the circuit judge get here quickly. He wants everything sorted out so the town can go back to normal and so Mr Tyler can finish his church."

For a moment, this was all beyond Gus. All he could think about was how much he hurt. "Am I shot bad?"

"Yes but luckily Mr Hobson was able to help Mr Tyler get the bullet out. They bandaged you up. Don't worry. Everything's fine now, really. I'll tell you all about it later on."

"Where's Jarrod?"

Myra bit her lip. That was the one piece of bad news amongst all the good. "He's in jail. That awful Mr Peabody was persuaded to wait until the Marshal got back but he just can't be persuaded to let Jarrod go. He's taking him back in the morning."

"Myra?"

"Yes?"

"You won't leave me will you?"

Myra's heart soared. "No. I'll be right by your side."

"Good." And smiling Gus closed his eyes and drifted back into sleep.

★ ★ ★

Jarrod lay in the cell next to that shared by Elmer and Bennett's wounded friend. They both moaned so much about their fates, the food and their wounds, that in a way he couldn't wait for the next day so that he could get away from them. Not that he wanted to go with Lester Peabody. It meant leaving Rock Springs, the good people he'd met and made friends with, leaving Brian Tyler; and Ginny. He didn't expect to see any of them again.

★ ★ ★

Brian Tyler tiptoed out of his room and into the corridor. He stood for a moment outside Lester Peabody's room. From inside he could hear the man snoring. If Peabody suffered any qualms of conscience about taking Jarrod back to Arizona, he certainly didn't let them affect his sleep. Still that suited Tyler.

At the bottom of the stairs Ginny waited for him. They grinned at one another like the conspirators they were.

"Ready?"

The girl nodded.

* * *

Although morning was still several hours away, Jarrod couldn't sleep. All he could do was wait. From the Marshal's office he heard the sound of a door opening and closing. A whispered conversation. He sat up. After a few moments the door to the cells opened. He peered into the dark, wondering who was being so furtive and why.

Two people came into the cells. One of them was carrying a lamp and by it he recognized Brian Tyler and Ginny!

He gaped at them in surprise. "What are you doing here?"

"Letting you out," Tyler said and opened the cell door. "Come on, hurry. Or don't you want to escape Peabody's clutches?"

"But you'll be in trouble," Jarrod protested.

"He'll be so anxious to catch up with you he won't bother with us," said Ginny.

"I'm not so sure about that."

"We are."

"What about Mr Cox? He could lose his job if anyone thinks he let me go."

"Unfortunately the poor Marshal did his duty and put up such severe resistance we had no choice but to tie him up."

But when Jarrod followed them into the office, he saw that the Marshal wasn't exactly tightly tied and although he wasn't gagged he wasn't making any noise to attract attention to the jailbreak.

"Your horse is outside," Tyler said. "There's food and clothes in the saddlebags. Your rifle and gun are loaded."

Jarrod hesitated. "I still don't like you doing this."

"It's our choice." Ginny flung herself into Jarrod's arms. "I wish you didn't have to go. I wish it had all turned out differently. But it hasn't and this is all we can do for you."

"Hurry up, Jarrod. You leave now and you'll have several hours' start on Peabody." Tyler grinned. "I can't wait to see his smug face when he realizes you've got away from him, again. Be careful, though, he won't give up unless he has to." The preacher reached out and shook the younger man's hand then gave him a quick hug. "I'll never forget you and what you did for me."

"I won't forget you either."

"I expect I shall be at Rock Springs

for the rest of my life so if you ever sort things out, be sure and come look me up."

"I will." Jarrod turned to Ginny again. Ginny was crying. They hugged tightly, both wondering if Jarrod would ever be able to sort his problems out. "I'll try to keep in touch."

"I expect I shall be here too."

"Thanks," Jarrod said to Marshal Cox.

The man nodded. "After what you did for the town I owe you. Besides, my wife would only have made my life a misery if I hadn't agreed to this."

Jarrod, Ginny and Tyler went outside. The town was quiet, the street lit by a pale moon shining above the trees.

There was nothing more to say and Jarrod got on his horse, kicking it into a trot. As he rode away, he kept looking back at the two figures, waiting and waving outside the jailhouse. The last time he looked he saw Ginny take hold of one of the preacher's hands and clutch it tightly.

FIGHTING RAMROD
Charles N. Heckelmann

Most men would have cut their losses, but Frazer counted the bullets in his guns and said he'd soak the range in blood before he'd give up another inch of what was his.

LONE GUN
Eric Allen

Smoke Blackbird had been away too long. The Lequires had seized the Blackbird farm, forcing the Indians and settlers off, and no one seemed willing to fight! He had to fight alone.

THE THIRD RIDER
Barry Cord

Mel Rawlins wasn't going to let anything stand in his way. His father was murdered, his two brothers gone. Now Mel rode for vengeance.

ARIZONA DRIFTERS
W. C. Tuttle

When drifting Dutton and Lonnie Steelman decide to become partners they find that they have a common enemy in the formidable Thurston brothers.

TOMBSTONE
Matt Braun

Wells Fargo paid Luke Starbuck to outgun the silver-thieving stagecoach gang at Tombstone. Before long Luke can see the only thing bearing fruit in this eldorado will be the gallows tree.

HIGH BORDER RIDERS
Lee Floren

Buckshot McKee and Tortilla Joe cut the trail of a border tough who was running Mexican beef into Texas. They stopped the smuggler in his tracks.

BRETT RANDALL, GAMBLER
E. B. Mann

Larry Day had the choice of running away from the law or of assuming a dead man's place. No matter what he decided he was bound to end up dead.

THE GUNSHARP
William R. Cox

The Eggerleys weren't very smart. They trained their sights on Will Carney and Arizona's biggest blood bath began.

THE DEPUTY OF SAN RIANO
Lawrence A. Keating and
Al. P. Nelson

When a man fell dead from his horse, Ed Grant was spotted riding away from the scene. The deputy sheriff rode out after him and came up against everything from gunfire to dynamite.

FARGO: MASSACRE RIVER
John Benteen

The ambushers up ahead had now blocked the road. Fargo's convoy was a jumble, a perfect target for the insurgents' weapons!

SUNDANCE: DEATH IN THE LAVA
John Benteen

The Modoc's captured the wagon train and its cargo of gold. But now the halfbreed they called Sundance was going after it . . .

HARSH RECKONING
Phil Ketchum

Five years of keeping himself alive in a brutal prison had made Brand tough and careless about who he gunned down . . .

FARGO: PANAMA GOLD
John Benteen

With foreign money behind him, Buckner was going to destroy the Panama Canal before it could be completed. Fargo's job was to stop Buckner.

FARGO: THE SHARPSHOOTERS
John Benteen

The Canfield clan, thirty strong were raising hell in Texas. Fargo was tough enough to hold his own against the whole clan.

PISTOL LAW
Paul Evan Lehman

Lance Jones came back to Mustang for just one thing — revenge! Revenge on the people who had him thrown in jail.

HELL RIDERS
Steve Mensing

Wade Walker's kid brother, Duane, was locked up in the Silver City jail facing a rope at dawn. Wade was a ruthless outlaw, but he was smart, and he had vowed to have his brother out of jail before morning!

DESERT OF THE DAMNED
Nelson Nye

The law was after him for the murder of a marshal — a murder he didn't commit. Breen was after him for revenge — and Breen wouldn't stop at anything . . . blackmail, a frameup . . . or murder.

DAY OF THE COMANCHEROS
Steven C. Lawrence

Their very name struck terror into men's hearts — the Comancheros, a savage army of cutthroats who swept across Texas, leaving behind a bloodstained trail of robbery and murder.

SUNDANCE: SILENT ENEMY
John Benteen

A lone crazed Cheyenne was on a personal war path. They needed to pit one man against one crazed Indian. That man was Sundance.

LASSITER
Jack Slade

Lassiter wasn't the kind of man to listen to reason. Cross him once and he'll hold a grudge for years to come — if he let you live that long.

LAST STAGE TO GOMORRAH
Barry Cord

Jeff Carter, tough ex-riverboat gambler, now had himself a horse ranch that kept him free from gunfights and card games. Until Sturvesant of Wells Fargo showed up.

McALLISTER ON THE COMANCHE CROSSING
Matt Chisholm

The Comanche, McAllister owes them a life — and the trail is soaked with the blood of the men who had tried to outrun them before.

QUICK-TRIGGER COUNTRY
Clem Colt

Turkey Red hooked up with Curly Bill Graham's outlaw crew. But wholesale murder was out of Turk's line, so when range war flared he bucked the whole border gang alone . . .

CAMPAIGNING
Jim Miller

Ambushed on the Santa Fe trail, Sean Callahan is saved by two Indian strangers. But there'll be more lead and arrows flying before the band join Kit Carson against the Comanches.

GUNSLINGER'S RANGE
Jackson Cole

Three escaped convicts are out for revenge. They won't rest until they put a bullet through the head of the dirty snake who locked them behind bars.

RUSTLER'S TRAIL
Lee Floren

Jim Carlin knew he would have to stand up and fight because he had staked his claim right in the middle of Big Ike Outland's best grass.

THE TRUTH ABOUT SNAKE RIDGE
Marshall Grover

The troubleshooters came to San Cristobal to help the needy. For Larry and Stretch the turmoil began with a brawl and then an ambush.